D1471708

Roy Pedersen was born in Ayrshire and brought up in Aberdeen. After a brief spell in London, where he created and published the first and best selling Gaelic map of Scotland, he has spent most of his working life based in Inverness. There he pursued a successful career in the economic, social and cultural development of the Highlands and Islands, and as an SNP Highland councillor. He writes, publishes, speaks and broadcasts in both English and Gaelic on a variety of issues connected with world affairs and with the history, present and future development of the "New Scotland" and its wider international setting.

i

OTHER BOOKS BY THE SAME AUTHOR

One Europe – A Hundred Nations
Loch Ness with Jacobite – A History of Cruising
on Loch Ness
Pentland Hero – The Story of the Orkney Short Sea
Crossing
George Bellairs – The Littlejohn Casebook: The 1940s

Roy Pedersen

DALMANNOCH
The Affair of Brother Richard

Pedersen
Lochlann
8 Drummond Road
Inverness
IV2 4NA

First published in Scotland in 2012

Pedersen
Lochlann
8 Drummond Road
Inverness
IV2 4NA
www.pedersen.org.uk

ISBN: 978-1-905787-68-5

This book is a work of fiction. The names characters,
organisations and incidents described are either imaginary
or are used fictitiously and no reference is made to any
living person.

British Library Cataloguing-in-Publication Data
A catalogue record for this book is available from the
British Library

Printed and bound by For the Right Reasons,
38 Grant Street, Inverness, IV3 8BN

For Davie

Dalmannoch – The Affair of Brother Richard

What is the link between a murdered lawyer and the growing love between a young monk and a nursing sister on the run from her violent husband? The action moves from the Cotswolds to Dalmannoch; a strange disused building in a remote corner of rural South West Scotland. A page-turner featuring a colourful and eccentric array of characters including: baffled police, a professor of Celtic, lawyers, neo-Pagans, Gaelic revivalists, a Canadian Laird and vile drug smuggling gangsters, all culminating in a thrilling climax.

CONTENTS   Page

*Map showing main places mentioned and the journey's of
Brother Richard and Sister Frances*

NEAR THE FAR SOUTH-WESTERN tip of Scotland in the rural province of Galloway, lies the ancient burgh of Wigtown. Had any of Wigtown's one thousand inhabitants been alert on that mid May Thursday afternoon, they would have seen two men crossing the broad Main Street.

One was well known and respected locally; the other a stranger. As they walked side by side, the younger and taller of the two seemed earnest in conveying some important point while the local man listened impassively. They made their way to a car parked in a side street and drove off, the younger man at the wheel; the older giving directions.

As it transpired the Wigtonites were too preoccupied with their own particular concerns that day to pay much attention to this apparently innocuous event. There was, however, no one but the two men themselves to witness what happened next.

Some twenty minutes after their departure from Wigtown, the pair stood in a secluded clearing beside a run-down building. The younger man was becoming irritated.

"Look, this place is a ruin. You won't get a better offer – or a better sweetener for yourself. It's too good to pass up, but unless I get your agreement here and now, the deal is off."

The older man was silent for a while; then he looked candidly at the other.

"Mr. – em – Arbuckle, as far as I am concerned, the deal, as you put it, has never been on. You say you have the agreement of the bishop in this matter, but I have had no such confirmation from him. As I have already indicated I am expecting to meet with a Brother Richard Wells, a monk from Whitleigh Priory in the Cotswolds. It is with him, and no one else, I am briefed to discuss the future of this property."

The younger man exploded in a rage at this point and grabbed the other's lapels.

"You stupid stubborn jackass! You bastard! You . . . !"

A brief tussle ensued. They both stumbled and fell over a sharp edged stone about the size of a pint mug. He grabbed the stone and smashed it down on the older man's forehead. It was a fatal blow.

BROTHER RICHARD was fond of Frances Flynn. It often crossed his mind that, in different circumstances, had it not been for his vows on entering holy orders, she was exactly the kind of woman with whom he would have wanted to settle down. He knew, of course, that a junior monk should turn aside such thoughts to contemplate instead other, more Godly affairs. That would certainly have been the view of Father John Ainslie, the formidable prior of Whitleigh Priory; a small Benedictine monastery on the edge of the Cotswold village of Wethercott St Giles.

Frances Flynn, or Sister Frances as she was known to her inmates, was manager-in-chief of the Meadow View Home for the Elderly. Thirty years old, attractive, brunette and trim of figure, her skirt was perhaps a mite shorter than might be expected of one in her position. But no one complained about that, among the men-folk at least. She moved with ease between managerial efficiency and a kindly word with her elderly charges. Estranged from a ne'er-do-well husband, her personal life had been fraught of late, but her competence as a nurse and her open human approach had eased her rapid rise through the ranks culminating in appointment to her current post.

Sister Frances liked Brother Richard's weekly visits to Meadow View. In fact she liked Brother Richard. She liked his quiet good humoured strength, his dark slightly wavy hair and those smouldering eyes that spoke of some heartbreak that had been overcome by a renewed purpose. Had he not been a monk, she thought . . .

That sunny April afternoon, Brother Richard smiled as he stuck his head round Sister Frances' office door on his accustomed Wednesday call. "How are our Meadow View crew today? – All ship-shape I hope?" He had been a sailor among other employment before joining the brothers at the priory and was at times inclined to lapse into nautical lingo.

The nurse turned from her report, flashed a welcoming smile as she met Brother Richard's eyes and, with her Donegal lilt replied; "Oh, the usual, but Mr. Bayliss isn't in good form. He was asking for you. How are things at Whitleigh?"

"Oh the usual," rejoined Brother Richard. "Making progress at last with the bell tower, now that the weather has picked up. You know, on a day like this the view from up there really lifts the spirits." Thus transpired the agreeable, if predictable, weekly ritual exchange between monk and nurse. "I'd better have a chat with Mr. Bayliss. See if I can buck him up."

Crossing the bright, cheerfully appointed, communal lounge, Brother Richard nodded to the familiar elderly residents one by one. Most seemed glad to see him. A few in their dotage looked blankly into space. Old Tom Bayliss, a character, if at times cantankerous, had been out of sorts for the last few days. He was sitting alone, eyes downcast, in a corner armchair.

"Well now Tom, how's it going? Looking a bit glum. What's up?"

The old man looked up at Brother Richard and offered a weak unconvincing smile – "Aw I'm all right, just got things on my mind". He went silent. Brother Richard sat beside him and waited. "It's me grandson, see. Me daughter Betty – you met 'er a couple o' months ago on one of her visits – she come ter see me on Sunday

4

an' told me about young Darren. He's gone off the rails. She's worried sick. He's a good lad, but you know what teenagers are like."

Brother Richard nodded. "I do. I was one once myself, and not that long ago."

"Th' thing is" Tom continued, "it seems he's gotten inter drugs. Running around wi' a bad lot. Betty doesn't know what to do, and neither do I – stuck here, out to grass, like an old cart horse. If only I could knock some sense inter the lad"

Brother Richard pondered for a minute. "Hm, I see. I can understand your concern – difficult state of affairs. Do you mind if I mention this to Sister Frances? She might be able to help."

Tom Bayliss considered for a while, his brow wrinkled – "Aw I don't suppose it would do any harm. She's a wise woman for her years. Maybe she could have a word with Betty." Tom's eyes seemed to brighten a little. "Thanks for listening Brother Richard, it's helped to share me troubles. You know, I haven't been much of a churchgoer but would you mind putting up a prayer for Darren? You'll have more influence with the almighty than an old sinner like me"

Brother Richard smiled, "Of course I will, but, you know, we're all sinners. Don't underestimate your own influence with God."

With the old countryman by his side, the young monk, prayed for the return of the injudicious youth to a straighter path and for relief of Tom's anxieties.

By the "Amen" old Tom, with a tear in his eye, took his comforter's hand and said, "God bless you Brother Richard; I have some hope now that things might get better."

5

Brother Richard rose; "God bless you too Tom. I'll speak with Sister".

A few more words of comfort here and words of cheer there to other Meadow View residents and Brother Richard made his way back to the manager-in-chief's office. As he approached a scream rang out – then:

"Ow! – Stop! – You're hurting me! – No Gerry – No!"

Brother Richard rushed into the office to witness Sister Frances, pinned to the wall by a highly agitated but smartly dressed fair haired man. "I'm due my share you bitch. I'm your husband."

"No Gerry" you have no right to it – Ow! The man had grabbed her violently under the neck and pushed her up the wall; his left hand was twisting her arm.

In an instant Brother Richard grabbed the assailant. "Oi! No you don't." he jerked the strangling right hand off Frances Flynn's neck. "Leave her be!"

Taken aback, the fair haired man released the Sister, turned round: "Bugger off! This is between me and my wife." He turned back to grab his victim again.

"Lay a finger on her", hissed Brother Richard, "and I'll deck you".

"You'll deck me? Don't make me laugh Holy Roller" and as a hand again made for the Sister's neck, the monk grabbed and twisted the attacker's arm, but he wriggled free and made a swing with his left fist at the 'Holy Roller'. Brother Richard ducked sustaining only a glancing blow on the upper cheek. He retaliated with a mighty right that knocked the fair haired man backwards, stumbling over a chair and on to the floor scattering the contents of the waste basket as he went down.

Furious, the downed man picked himself up. "You've asked for it now" and he took a swing with his right which again with surprising dexterity, Brother Richard avoided, to respond with a well aimed right of his own, then a left hook and another smashing right, such that the unwelcome visitor sank stunned to the ground with blood oozing from his mouth and nose.

"Holy Roller I may be, but no one violates a woman in my presence" he held the dazed man in a half-Nelson and, turning to Sister Frances, asked, "Who is this apology for a man?"

"That apology for a man – that snake – is my husband Gerry", retorted the sister still trembling as she started to recover from her ordeal. "I left him a year ago – thank God – and now he's after me for money. If I never see him again, it'll be too soon."

With that Brother Richard pulled Gerry Flynn to his feet and frog marched him to the front door of the normally tranquil Meadow View Home for the Elderly and unceremoniously, and to the surprise of a couple of arriving visitors, flung him out sprawled on the gravel with the warning: "Come within a mile of Frances and I'll not be so gentle with you next time."

As he picked himself up, Gerry Flynn retorted, "I'll not forget this Holy Roller" and slunk off through the car park, nursing his aching face.

"Wow!" exclaimed a still breathless Frances Flynn when Brother Richard returned through the front door, "I never knew monks could handle themselves in a fight like that."

"Oh," sighed Brother Richard, "it's just something I picked up in a former life."

With that the Sister-in-chief threw her arms round the startled monk. "Thank you, thank you so much. I don't know what would have happened if you hadn't been around."

Comforting her, Brother Richard put his arms around her waist and kissed her brow. He felt the grateful woman's firm breasts pressing against him as she kissed his mouth.

A voice boomed: "What in God's name is going on". It was Father John, Prior of Whitleigh.

The kiss that landed Brother Richard in trouble

PENANCE

W HEN THE RUCKUS at Meadow View had started, Sharon Wilkins, the senior care assistant had telephoned the priory to say that Brother Richard was in trouble and to send urgent assistance; hence the prior's arrival on the scene. This well intentioned action had the unfortunate end result that Brother Richard found himself in deeper trouble than the simple matter of a set to with Gerry Flynn.

That Father John was displeased at the sight of one of his brothers in kissing embrace with an attractive young woman, after the same brother had been involved in a brawl, may be regarded as understating his attitude. He was incensed. The explanation, that Brother Richard had intervened to save a damsel in dire distress and had then sought to comfort her, cut little ice with the Prior.

Father John Ainslie, a tall austere Yorkshire man, was well known as the visionary leader who had worked near miracles to develop the priory of Whitleigh from a state of virtual insolvency to become a productive monastic house, famed for its Whitleigh Mead and its illuminated Gospel texts. His view was unambiguous. Monks were chaste men of piety and peace and that was the foundation on which the priory was based. Any lesser standard was unacceptable and that was that.

There had to be atonement. Brother Richard was confined to the priory. There would be strict observance of the canonical hours and additional religious study. No contact with Meadow View was permitted and certainly not with Frances Flynn. Brother Sylvester would henceforth take over the role of comforter to the elderly residents. Work on the bell tower would, however, continue for Prior John was realistic enough to recognise the worth of Brother Richard's considerable building skills.

Obedience is a central tenet of monastic life and, in a real effort to make amends; Brother Richard threw himself into his work on the priory's bell tower which was now well advanced. His father Robert Wells had been a jobbing builder and his inquisitive offspring Nick, as Brother Richard was then known, had absorbed many of the fundamentals of the building trade as he had pottered about his father's yard. On leaving school, he had spent three years as an apprentice joiner before his life took a different course. Not just one course but a series of paths, scrapes, adventures, tragedies until here he was, at the age of thirty three, Brother Richard, a junior monk in the Priory of Whitleigh, deep in what many would regard as a rural Cotswold idyll.

He had come on Whitleigh by chance and had at once been attracted by the peace and stability of the monastic life he observed there, and especially attracted to the musical tradition, for at Whitleigh Mass and choral services are conducted in Latin. His strong singing voice took readily to Gregorian chant. After several visits to Whitleigh he had committed himself to the stages of postulancy, after that the two year noviciate, and then eventually after study of monastic tradition, scripture, liturgy and much else, had, six months before, being allowed to take temporary vows. At this point he was given the new name Richard and received the white habit and scapular of the order. It would be a further two and half years before he would take his Solemn Vows to commit fully to the monastic life, if such he decided to do and if the brothers voted to accept him. While the monastic life held great attraction, it was not always easy to live up to the requirements of the Benedictine rule. Brother Richard, aka Nick Wells, had not previously been strongly religious and had indeed been brought up somewhat passively as a Methodist. His conversion to Catholicism had been fairly recent. The spirituality of 'Peter's crew' had undoubtedly moved him but, try as he did, at times he found aspects of the theology difficult to grasp.

In the main, the Brothers had been welcoming and helpful although, at times, Brother Richard sensed undercurrents – petty jalousies, self-righteousness, obsequiousness. One brother in particular, Brother Jacob, the Priory's Store Master, seemed to exhibit all of these tendencies, not strongly but, in such a way that Brother Richard felt slightly uncomfortable about the other's probing enquiries as to what he was doing and how he was managing. In his previous life, however, Nick Wells had dealt with a wide range of rum characters, by comparison with which, the monks appeared as paragons.

The penance ensuing from the incident at Meadow View was a set back. Brother Richard couldn't help but feel a nagging sense of injustice although he tried hard to put that thought aside. At least from his perch high on the bell tower the broad prospect below and around him seemed to extend his thoughts away from his troubles. From that height he could see the village of Wethercott St Giles, golden in its weathered Cotswold stone, serene with its square towered parish church. Beyond lay rolling farmland interspersed with woodland and cottages, formerly of farm servants, and now mainly weekend retreats or retirement homes for the urban middle classes. The sky was blue with only a few wispy clouds casting slow moving shadows across that English chocolate box pastoral landscape.

11

It was in this appealing setting, as he laid stone on stone, that he recalled his happy youthful days in Brixham before the terrible car crash in which his parents and younger brother Nigel had died. He thought about his Cornish mother Martha Trelawney, who had hailed originally from Newlyn, and of the many blissful holidays with his grandparents at that busy fishing port.

Then he thought about school. He had hated it, although oddly he enjoyed Latin, maths and music. His teachers said he had a good brain but didn't try. Neither had he much interest in team games, preferring to spend his time sailing, fishing or listening to the yarns of the Brixham fishermen. After the trauma of his parents' death, his aunt and uncle took him in and fixed up an apprenticeship.

Bullied by one of the older lads, he joined a gym to learn boxing. This soon put an end to the bullying. Then the collapse of the building company put an end to the apprenticeship.

As his reverie unfolded, he glanced over to the Meadow View building which was clearly visible, just quarter of a mile away on the edge of the village. There standing by the doorway was Sister Frances speaking with some visiting relatives. As the visitors departed, Frances Flynn looked in the direction of the priory, shaded her eyes, and then, spotting Brother Richard high on the bell tower, waved. Brother Richard waved back. A tingle of elation raised his spirits for the first time since that day almost two weeks before when everything had gone wrong. The sense of joy was followed by a pang of guilt. Could a wave across a quarter mile void be regarded as contact?

With this thought he suddenly remembered Tom Bayliss. There had been no opportunity to appraise Sister

Frances about the old man's concerns. How could that be done now that communications were cut? How remiss to leave such a matter unsettled. Perhaps there was little the Meadow View manager-in-chief could do to resolve the problems of a mother and son whom she hardly knew. But still some effort should be made. The answer to the conundrum came in the shape of Brother Sylvester, the shy kindly monk who, while lacking the worldly experience of Brother Richard, was now the main contact between priory and Meadow View.

That evening at Vespers, there was a brief opportunity to speak with Brother Sylvester to explain the anxiety Tom Bayliss harboured for his daughter and grandson. Brother Sylvester agreed that on the following day, being a Wednesday, and the day scheduled for his Meadow View visit, he would pass on this intelligence to Sister Frances.

That night Brother Richard fell asleep with one of his beloved Gregorian psalms in his inner ear, dreaming of his south coast youth and of Frances Flynn.

F RANCES FLYNN had been shaken by her husband's violent assault. Brother Richard's intervention had saved the day but at a cost. Her instinctive display of gratitude and affection had resulted in that lovely strong man being confined to barracks, for that is how she now saw the Priory of Whitleigh. How embarrassing. How unfair.

Over the week following this harrowing incident, a kind of normality resumed in the operation of Meadow View, apart from the irritation that the disturbance had been reported to the trustees. This necessitated a report on the circumstances and some reassurance that such an event was not likely to reoccur. The appearance of Brother Sylvester on the ensuing Wednesday, however, confirmed that normality was not as it used to be. The elderly residents felt it too, notwithstanding Brother Sylvester's sympathetic and well-meant administrations. No one said as much, but Brother Richard was missed.

At the same time as Brother Richard had been recalling his youth and the paths he had followed, Frances Flynn – Frances McGarrigle as she then was – remembered her own happy childhood in County Donegal where her father Sean had taught in Letterkenny. She thought especially fondly of the regular visits and holidays in the far west to Gweedore, the home territory of her Irish Gaelic speaking mother, Nuala O'Brien, where she and her brother Finbarr were allowed to run wild. Later, as with so many of County Donegal's sons and daughters on leaving school, she crossed the Irish Sea to Liverpool where she started training as a nurse. She enjoyed nursing and the city life in equal measure.

She worked hard, played hard. Life was fun then. She brought to mind the succession of boy-friends of varying provenence, who had enriched her experience, if not necessarily her piety, for the unwelcome lewd advances of her priest had put an end to any diminishing interest in church attendance.

Then she recalled that, as a fully fledged nurse, the social whirl calmed down while her dedication and hard work had earned her plaudits. After a few years she moved to a promoted post in Bristol. Promotion aside, Bristol was where her favourite aunt Mary lived. Mary McGarrigle, a former music teacher was Frances' late father's older, slightly eccentric, and by then elderly, unmarried sister. Bristol was also where Frances met Gerry Flynn.

Gerry was a quick witted charmer, good looking some five years her senior with his own semi-detached house in one of Bristol's new-build housing developments. He was a car salesman with the Bristol based francise Abona Motors, a company with several outlets around the Severn area. Successful in this capacity, he was generally seen driving one of the showroom's fancier models: one week a BMW cabriolet; the next a Range Rover. The courtship was a short one and within a year the pair were married and she, Senior Staff Nurse Frances McGarrigle, became Mrs. Flynn. After that, what had started as a fun affair deteriorated bit by bit into an unhappy mismatch of a level-headed woman advancing in her career and an unreliable man with a penchant for gambling, usually at a place in Bristol called the Casino de Oro. She shuddered as she relived those best efforts to find a feasible *modus vivendi*, only to be thwarted by Gerry's financial irresponsibilty, suspicious trips away and increasingly violent outbursts

15

resulting eventually in her walking out and moving in
briefly with her ailing aunt.

The post of manager-in-chief of the Meadow
View Home for the Elderly had been advertised just
before the marital separation and Frances had seen it as
an ideal opportunity to make a fresh start in a responsible
position with the added attraction of live-in
accommodation provided. And so it proved. Five months
after she had taken up the new post, Aunt Mary died
leaving her estate jointly to Frances and Finbarr. As
Finbarr lived and worked in Dublin, it fell mainly to
Frances to handle the business of selling the house, most
of its contents and winding up the estate. In so doing,
each sibling inherited £214,000. It was a goodly slice of
this that Gerry sought to pay off his gambling debts.

* * *

Having pondered this chain of life-time events,
Sister Frances set to her duties with her usual courteous
efficiency. It was after escorting two relatives of one of
the more senile residents to Meadow View's front door
that she looked over to Whitleigh Priory, as she often did,
and there high on the bell tower she spied Brother
Richard. She held her hand to her forehead to shade her
eyes. Was he looking over at Meadow View? She waved.
He waved back. That felt better – much better – but
better still if only they could meet face to face.

Next day, as arranged, Brother Sylvester
delivered Brother Richard's message about Tom Bayliss'
grandson and his drugs issue. Sister Frances spoke with
Tom, confirmed his concerns. To seek advice, she
phoned Nancy Smythe, a former colleague, now a social
worker in Gloucester.

16

"It's a problem that's all too common" confided Nancy, "and it's not so easy to find effective solutions. It depends a lot on the individual and his willingness to tackle his problem. There are quite a number of drug rehabilitation programs. Maybe the best thing would be to meet the lad and his mother to get a better idea of what's what and then we could see what can be done. I can contact a youth worker for the family's area. He's a good man – Jack Springer – an ex footballer."

Sister Frances phoned Tom Bayliss' daughter Betty Williams to suggest a visit on the pretext of bringing her up to date with Tom's circumstances. It was not until the following week that her work schedule allowed her the time to drive over to Cirencester where careworn Betty lived in a council flat.

"It's nice to see you Betty. I know its not easy for you to manage over very often to Meadow View to see your father. I though I'd just take the chance when I was passing through to let you know how he is." The two women sat over coffee.

"It's good of you to call Sister. I know I should try to visit more often but I am on my own and what with my shifts at the supermarket and the buses and my boy Darren, it's not easy."

"I know Betty. In fact it's Darren I wanted to talk to you about. Your father's worried about him and I wondered if I could help."

"I know Dad's worried. I'm worried sick. I don't know what to do. Darren's in with a bad crowd and – and drugs. I can't reason with him. If only somebody could do something."

With that there was the rattle of a key in the front door and Darren walked in – a youth of seventeen in standard teenager garb of tee-shirt, trackie bottoms, trainers and hoodie sweatshirt.

"Darren this is Sister Frances from Meadow View. She's telling me about Granddad."

"Cool" was the youth's response. Then after a shrug and an awkward pause: "Is he OK?" Darren was fond of his grandfather.

Sister Frances broke in: "He's not too bad. He cares a lot about you, you know. He'd love you to visit him."

"Cool."

"He tells me you're a good footballer."

"Used to play a bit at school – but . . ." Despite his awkwardness Darren had taken a bit of a shine to Sister Frances. "Yeah, I quite like football."

"Well, before you go to see your Granddad, there's someone I'd like you to meet. His name's Joe Springer. He was striker with . . ."

And that in a nutshell is how Frances Flynn set in course a plan to try to steer Darren on to a straighter path.

On hearing this Tom Bayliss bucked up and about ten days later Darren paid him a visit. On Sister Frances advice, the matter of drugs was not discussed while the matter of football was dwelt on at length. Joe Springer had apparently got Darren involved in a training programme. Tom and Sister Frances knew that there was no guarantee of success but the signs were hopeful.

It was a Tuesday, a few days after Darren's visit, that Sister Frances called again to see Betty. It was early days, but Betty seemed more hopeful than on the previous call. As they discussed progress over coffee, Sister Frances' mobile phone rang.

"Excuse me a minute. Let me see who this is." Sister Frances held the instrument to her ear: "Hello?"

The voice at the other end was that of Sharon Wilkins, the senior care assistant at Meadow View.

"Sorry to bother you Sister, but your husband's at Meadow View. He's raging and swearing and demanding to see you !"

B ROTHER RICHARD; I want to have a word with you. Come to my study after Terce tomorrow." Did Prior John's command have a hint of a threat or was it just that his grave Yorkshire manner always seemed to convey some sense of weighty import?

A week had passed since Brother Sylvester had passed on the concerns of Tom Bayliss and who, on return, had mentioned discreetly to Brother Richard that Sister Frances had asked him to convey to him her thanks and best regards and that she would look into the matter of Tom's grandson. Had word about this minor infringement of the 'no contact' prohibition reached the ears of Prior John?

Terce is one of the 'small' canonical hours after Mass at about nine in the morning when a short service is attended by the brothers. In response to the Prior's summons, Brother Richard made his way through the cloister; passed the chapter house and slype to ascend the stairway to the door of the prior's study. The solid oak door bore a varnished name plate with the words in gilt letters:

DOM JOHN AINSLIE
PRIOR

"Enter!" came the command in response to Brother Richard's knock. The young monk complied. The book lined study overlooked the cloister and, seated behind a battered but substantial oak desk laden with documents, the prior looked up and leaned back on his chair.

"Take a seat Richard." A hand was wafted in the direction of a chair facing the prior at the front of the desk. Brother Richard sat down, apprehensive as to what criticism might be forthcoming. The prior's expression was impossible to read, but then it almost always was. He paused as if thinking how best to express his thoughts.

At length he spoke. "You have made good progress with the bell tower."

"Well yes Father – thank you" responded Brother Richard, with some relief although wondering what was coming next. He added; "the masonry is now up to full height. We are just about ready to put the roof in place".

"Quite," concurred the Prior; "quite – yes indeed. Your building skills, and if I may say, the quality of your work, have been an asset to Whitleigh."

Brother Richard, in his relief, didn't know quite what to say but managed to mutter "thank you – I – em – have tried to do as good a job as I could".

"Quite – quite", said the Prior, just a little impatiently, "however, I have something different in mind for you for the next while".

At this Brother Richard's new found sense of relief evaporated and a fresh cloud of misgiving joined his fluctuating emotions.

Prior John leaned forward with his elbows on the desk and placed the tips of his fingers together in front of his mouth, pondered for half a minute and then spoke. "I had better explain."

"There's a place in Scotland called – let me see," the prior consulted a letter on his desk, "ah yes; it's called Dalmannoch. There exists there a building that in the past functioned as a Catholic retreat but has been

21

disused for some years. Now there are a number of peculiar things about this building and its grounds. As I understand it, the land on which it stands, which is, I am told, in a relatively remote rural area, was gifted by some nineteenth century landowner. He also provided the funds for its erection and created a trust to own and operate it. The terms and structure of the trust are odd, but I won't go into that just now. Suffice it to say that one of the trustees is our own Bishop Newman and he has asked for my help."

"As I said, the building hasn't been used for quite a while and is in poor shape. The Bishop believes that the most desirable outcome would be to sell the whole thing. In that event, the Bishop has indicated that this monastic foundation could be a beneficiary of the proceeds. One of the difficulties is that the building can't simply be sold on the open market to anyone. The terms of the trust require that it be sold as a functioning spiritual endeavour – ah hem – as a going concern, as it were. This is where I have a very important role for you Richard".

Brother Richard was flabbergasted. What on earth could he do about some tumbledown edifice in some backwater enveloped in some obscure legal wrangle? He had been a joiner, boxer, fisherman, sailor, builder and was now a junior monk, not yet ready to take his Solemn Vows. He knew little about the law and knew nothing of Scotland.

As these thoughts infiltrated Brother Richard's increasingly confused mind, Prior John continued: "You may be wondering what exactly I have in mind for you and indeed why I have chosen you Richard."

Brother Richard was stuck for words. "Damned right I am" he thought irreverently and guiltily, but could only utter the words: "well – em – well – yes. What is it you want me to do? I'm not sure if I . . ."

"Quite, quite," Prior John continued, "I can understand your – er – perplexity. Firstly, the reason I have chosen you, is that you are a junior monk who has not yet taken his Solemn Vows. I want a young and resourceful man to undertake this task. And as young monks go you have had more worldly experience than most. Furthermore you have a practical bent not least with building work and you are personable. The last named attribute, I fear, at times detracts from your piety, but for the task in view, it will be an advantage. What I want you to do is this."

"I want you to go to Dal . . ." the Prior looked again at the letter on his desk, "ah yes, Dalmannoch. I want you to tidy the building up, if possible pulling in some local voluntary help to aid you, and I want you to get to know the area and the people with a view to finding some prospective buyer of a spiritual nature. It is a big responsibility, I know, but you will be given a vehicle, tools and a small fund for materials and food. Fortunately the summer is approaching and it will not be too much of a hardship for you to sleep in the building. This will be a test not only of your resourcefulness but it will also give you time to think about your vocation as a monk – one way or the other.

We will work out your requirements over the next few days and I will expect you to be on your way to Scotland in the next couple of weeks or so.

THE BELL TOWER AND OTHER MATTERS

O N THE FOLLOWING three days, Brother Richard, with the assistance of three other monks, Brothers: Matthew, Wilfred and Brendan, completed the bell tower's masonry work and secured in place the heavy bell-frame and trunnions that would support the bell itself. The bell, which had come from a demolished Anglican church in the East End of London, had been bought some five years before for a knock down price at auction by one of Prior John's many contacts. All that remained to complete the tower was the installation of the bell and the placing of the roof over the structure.

Brother Richard had marvelled at the builders of old, perched high and precariously on the pinnacle of some steeple, putting the last slates and finial in place, with nothing but fresh air between them and a deadly drop of a hundred feet or more. He was grateful that he was not faced with that prospect, for over the inclement winter months, he had prefabricated the roof at ground level under the direction of Whitleigh's architect Jamie Arbuckle. This talented, if irascible, young Scotsman, whose office was located in the trendy Leith Shore area of Edinburgh, was starting to make a name for himself in ecclesiastical restorations. He had been especially pleased to have been commissioned to design, along traditional lines, and oversee the construction of the new bell tower. He was less pleased at the reduced fee negotiated by Prior John.

A week later the crane arrived. Devotions were suspended and the prior and his brothers watched from below as first the bell and then the roof were lifted and lowered to their respective positions. Brothers Richard, Matthew, Wilfred and Brendan were on high to grab the heavy swinging bell with its headstock and wheel, and, in concert with Jamie Arbuckle's signals to the crane-man, the brothers eased the assembly into place between its trunnions. Next came the prefabricated roof – even heavier and acting as a lethal pendulum in the light breeze. The brothers grabbed it, steadied it and bit by bit guided it towards its seatings. Brother Richard held his breath. He was confident that he had measured everything correctly, and yet . . . Down, slowly, down – then contact. It was square and true; not more than a centimetre proud of its marks – not too bad for a joiner who hadn't finished his apprenticeship!

Jamie Arbuckle checked the corners and edges. "Excellent! Well within tolerances. Let's get it clipped down and secure." As Brothers Wilfred and Brendan attended to these finishing touches, Brother Richard attached the bell rope to the wheel as Brother Matthew lowered the tail-end of the rope down through the tower to the ringing chamber far below. By the time those on high had descended to join the Prior and the other brothers on the ground, there was a buzz of excitement. Prior John led the blessing with words of an appropriate and holy nature and then Dom Anthony, Whitleigh's oldest monk, was given the honour of ringing the bell for the first time in its new setting. As it rang out sweetly, an unspoken sense of approval, contentment, and, it has to be admitted, pride prevailed among those gathered at the foot of the new tower. The tolling of the bell was of course a signal for all to repair to the chapel for Mass, thanksgiving and for the routine of monastic life to resume.

Over those ten days the completing of the bell tower had been a major preoccupation for Brother Richard; a project in whose technicalities, while challenging, he felt confident. There was, on the other hand, the matter of preparing for the expedition to Scotland. On that he was not comfortable. Things became a little clearer, however, when Prior John had called him in for another meeting.

"Now Richard, I am able to give you some more information about the task you will undertake in Scotland. Firstly the trust that owns the land and building at Dalmannoch is called The Dalmannoch Trust. I understand that there are three trustees: our own bishop, a Canadian gentleman called Hector Woodrow-Douglas and a local law firm in the nearby town Wigtown represented by a Mr. Alexander Agnew. He will be able to advise you when you arrive at Dalmannoch. Apparently it was an ancestor of Mr. Woodrow-Douglas who had gifted the land on which the Dalmannoch chapel and seminary was built and as it happens the family also had ancestral land here around Wethercott St Giles."

Prior John paused, and then referring to a document on his desk continued, "It seems that the trust deeds are very specific about the conditions under which the Dalmannoch chapel and seminary can be disposed of. If sold, the property must continue to be used for the spiritual enlightenment of the inhabitants of Galloway (that is the far south-western part of Scotland) and, the proceeds from the sale must be used for the development of a Roman Catholic foundation in lands around Wethercott St Giles as defined in a plan attached to the trust deed. The only such foundation that fulfils that definition is this Priory of Whitleigh. You will understand, Richard, the importance of an injection of funds to our work here."

Brother Richard looked candidly at the prior. "I do see that. I know the bell tower has stretched our finances to the limit." He reflected for a while. "Without seeing the building, it's difficult to know what may be required. But I suppose, given the right equipment and some help, I can possibly get the place spruced up. It's just . . . I'm not sure I can . . . I'm not sure I have the skills to find a suitable buyer – a buyer who's in the business of, how did you put it 'spiritual enlightenment'."

"I think you will surprise yourself Richard." The Prior was unwavering. "The Bishop tells me that Mr. Agnew will be helpful and has many contacts. He has been able to release some modest funds from the trust, so Brother Jacob has managed to acquire a van through one of his contacts at the Abona Motors branch in Cheltenham. It's a somewhat elderly vehicle, but will serve you adequately and Brother Jacob will provide you with a selection of tools and equipment from our store here. Once you have had a chance to spruce the place up a bit, I have arranged for Jamie Arbuckle to check the place over and to advise you as to what repairs or modifications may be required prior to disposal."

Prior John rummaged in his desk drawer and drew out a sealed envelope. "Here is a description of how to get to Dalmannoch once you are in Scotland, the keys to the chapel and other buildings and £500 to cover fuel and other expenses. Mr. Agnew will meet you when you arrive at Dalmannoch and he will arrange further finance and advice once you have established yourself there.

* * *

It was with a heavy heart that Brother Richard made final preparations for this daunting enterprise. On the last day before his departure Brother Jacob had been given leave to spend a few days with his ailing mother who was terminally ill. His absence meant that Brother Richard had to undertake the final loading of the van himself, a task that he undertook with little enthusiasm. His mood was not improved that night, by the news from Brother Sylvester that Sister Frances Flynn had suddenly left Meadow View and had left no forwarding address.

THE JOURNEY NORTH

THAT THURSDAY MORNING of Brother Richard's departure was grey and overcast. It was a little after nine before the old Ford Transit panel van was fully loaded. Several of the monks gathered to wish Brother Richard a safe journey and success with his quest.

Prior John himself had the last word, "God be with you my son. He will guide you and support you through any troubles you may encounter". Wise man, though he was, little did the Prior realise just what troubles lay ahead.

Brother Richard half turned the ignition key, waited a few seconds then turned it fully and, with a cough, the two and a half litre diesel engine burst into life. Gear selected, clutch released and in his rear-view mirror Brother Richard saw the waving monks disappear as he turned out of the monastery grounds and on to the national road network.

Although ten years old with almost 125,000 miles on the clock, the van was newly serviced. It was surprisingly comfortable and easy to drive. Of course it had no such luxury as 'sat-nav' but with an up to date road atlas on the passenger seat, the route to the north was easy enough to follow. Through the rolling Cotswolds at first, then after about forty minutes the sign "Midlands" led on to the M5 Motorway. By this time it had started to drizzle. The wipers squeaked on the backstroke. The rain became heavier. The wipers still squeaked and the spray thrown up from fast moving heavy trucks and a misting windscreen called for full concentration to see the road ahead. As he negotiated the

29

right hand lane to join the M6 following the sign "The North West", Brother Richard felt both tense and thoroughly miserable.

This despondency was heightened by puzzlement at Sister Frances' disappearance and a feeling of powerlessness as to how he might help, if help were needed. Was her delinquent husband involved? That man who had got him into such trouble with the prior.

That thought turned his mind to Prior John himself and his motives. Why had the prior chosen him, rather than one of the more experienced brothers, to undertake this baffling task in the north? It felt as though he was being put to some kind of impossible fool's errand – a set-up in which he was the fall guy. But why?

As he tossed these gloomy reflections around his brain, he was less aware than he should have been that there is a kind of mind numbing monotony about motorway driving that can lull the unwary into going faster than is wise. Direction signs and service areas become totems of progress inspiring the urge to press on and on. On the outside lane at 85 miles an hour vehicle after vehicle was left behind until a Massive articulated truck pulled out to pass another truck just as the Ford van was overtaking. Screech of brakes – skid – swerve, Brother Richard fought to bring the van under control on the wet carriageway. The driver of the big truck, realising what he had done, pulled back and, with pounding heart, the monk squeezed the van through the now widening gap. That was too close for comfort. A lesson was learnt. Keep the speed down to 70 maximum.

It took some minutes for the adrenalin rush to subside. Why not try the radio? A couple of raucous music stations – not what was required – then Classic

FM. That would do. Mozart improved Brother Richard's frame of mind.

"Settle down", he thought. "We've a long way to go." Quite who 'we' was is an open question, but he wondered about what Scotland might have in store. He had never been north of the border although he had sailed with Scottish shipmates from Glasgow, Aberdeen and softly spoken men from what were referred to as 'The Islands'. A mixed, but by and large a friendly bunch. As a mariner, he was aware that his destination was only three degrees of latitude north of Whitleigh Priory, but he had the foreboding notion that the Scottish weather would be very different from his native West Country – cold, wet, windy; snow bound perhaps? If the rain was this heavy passing the Stafford service area, what was it going to be like further north?

The rain poured from the heavens, the wipers maintained their unrelenting squeak and service areas passed one by one – Keele; Sandbach; Knutsford. By Lymm the rain stopped. By Lancaster a watery sun was trying to show face behind the van, the traffic thinned and soon the hills of Cumbria lay ahead. As the motorway curved and climbed among the enveloping fells, Brother Richard's spirits lifted. He felt suddenly hungry and thirsty in need of a pee and what's more the fuel gauge was now around the half full mark. He pulled off at the Tebay service area. From past experience, Brother Richard had no great love of motorway service stops with their overpriced processed food, soulless atmosphere and it seemed soulless clientele under the power of some soulless corporation.

Pleasant surprise. Tebay was different. Locally owned, locally sourced food, friendly staff and even moderately cheerful customers. The salad and fruit juice was most acceptable; the window seat beside a pond set off by views over the Westmorland Fells was a bonus.

"Mind if I share your table?" A well dressed man in early middle age holding a tray with a plate of chicken curry and a glass of fizzy cola gestured at the place opposite.

"Oh, by all means. Please take a seat."

"Thank you."

After setting out his plate, glass and cutlery before him, the stranger smiled a pleasant smile: "Where are you heading?"

"To Galloway – a place not far from Whithorn."

"Well, well, quite a coincidence, so am I – not exactly Whithorn, but Newton Stewart."

"Is that near Whithorn?" enquired Brother Richard.

"Well yes, it's only about twenty miles away. Is this your first visit?"

"Yes it is. It'll be my first visit to Scotland altogether."

"Oh, I'm sure you'll love it. Whithorn is an interesting little town and the Machars are a beautiful unspoilt area full of history. Are you on holiday?"

"Well no, not exactly. I'm a monk from Whitleigh Priory in the Cotswolds and I have to – how can I say – I have been given some work to do at a place called Dalmannoch."

"Well, well, well – how interesting. I don't think I have ever met a real live monk before. I thought you had to wear a – a – cloak, or is it a habit?"

"Yes, a habit, and I do at Whitleigh, but while I'm out on an assignment of this sort I wear everyday clothes."

"Well, well; come to think of it, it's the same with me. I'm a lawyer so when I'm in court, I wear a wig and gown; otherwise I go about in civvies. I've heard of Dalmannoch – a former Catholic establishment, I believe, but closed down for some years now."

"Yes that's right. In fact I expect to be met by a lawyer, later this afternoon at Dalmannoch – a Mr. Agnew."

"Ah yes Alexander Agnew of Agnew, Douglas and McWhirter. You'll be alright with him. He's an old style country solicitor and very sound. Always wears a tweed suit and white carnation in his button-hole. He's known by some as AA, like Alcoholics Anonymous, although he's a life-long teetotaler ! My name, by the way, is Robert Heron. Here's my card. You won't need me professionally if you have Alec to look after you, but look me up sometime, I'd be interested to hear how you get on at Dalmannoch. Meantime I recommend you take your time through Galloway and enjoy the scenery. By the way if I may correct your pronunciation; the final 'ch' is not pronounced 'ck' but as in our Scottish 'Loch' and the stress is on the middle syllable. We say 'dal MAN och'."

"Thank you for the correction. I shall try to get it right. My name's Richard – Richard Wells. They call me Brother Richard. It was nice meeting you, but I must get going now. I don't want to keep Mr. Agnew, or should I say AA, waiting. I hope we meet again." With that Brother Richard bid his farewell to head back to the van. And he felt strangely happy.

The exit from the car park led past a fuel station – "but not at that price" thought Brother Richard. "What would Prior John say?" Monk and van proceeded northwards at a more relaxed pace and about half an hour later, just past the turn off for Carlisle, he filled up with diesel for a much more reasonable price. As the van crossed the border into Scotland the sun shone in a blue blue sky, he followed the sign 'South West Scotland, Dumfries, Gretna, Stranraer' off the M6 to merge on to the A75. Westwards he travelled, past Annan, Dumfries, Castle Douglas, where-after the landscape changed from pleasant pastoral to a grander hillier aspect and now coastal views reminiscent of the English South Coast of which he had such happy childhood memories. At the Newton Stewart junction, he stopped and consulted the instructions supplied by Alexander Agnew. With the note spread out on the passenger seat, he set off south this time by the A714, to by-pass Wigtown and thence a series of by-roads eventually to turn off, at a peeling 'Dalmannoch' sign, along a narrow curved drive through a small patch of woodland. And there, on the shoulder of a slight rise, lay the little chapel, residential and out buildings of Dalmannoch.

It was a few minutes before five o'clock. Brother Richard stopped the van with the engine running, just short, to take in the scene. The vegetation was overgrown and although the stone buildings had a neglected air, they looked sound enough and indeed, despite being boarded up, surprisingly picturesque in the late afternoon sun. Then he drew the van up to the chapel, pulled on the brake, switched off the engine and stepped down from the Transit – head still buzzing from the noise of the engine. The warm air bore the scent of some sweet herb, myrtle perhaps, a cock blackbird sang from the top of the chapel gable. And through a gap in the trees, lay a rolling landscape of green fields and grazing cattle. Not at all as bad as he had feared, he thought; not bad at all.

Brother Richard took the keys from the envelope and made his way round the gable end of the chapel to the door of the accommodation building and there on the ground, face down, lay a man – a man in a tweed suit. As Brother Richard approached the motionless figure, he could see blood was oozing from the forehead. The monk knelt down and felt for a pulse. There was none. A white carnation peeped from under the lapel of the tweed jacket.

THE NEWS that her husband was once again back at Meadow View and on her tail came as a shock to Frances Flynn. Her mind raced as she took in the import of Sharon Wilkins' message.

"Are you still there came the voice at the other end?"

"Yes, yes – sorry I need to think. Look, tell him I'm away overnight. Tell him there's no point in him staying. If he doesn't go, call the police. I'll phone you in a couple of hours once he's out the way and once I've had a chance to collect my thoughts."

Darren's mother Betty looked quizzically at Sister Frances. "I'm sorry" said the nurse, "I'm afraid there's a bit of a problem at Meadow View. I'll need to make some phone calls to sort things out." She rose to leave: "But I'm glad Darren seems to be responding to Joe Springer's regime. Don't be too disheartened if there are set backs now and again but, with a bit of luck, Joe'll straighten Darren out."

With that Frances bade farewell to Betty and drove to The Brewery Car Park near the centre of Cirencester. Walking absent-mindedly up to the Market Place she was oblivious to the venerable St John the Baptist church that dominates the historic Cotswold town or indeed to any of its other attractions. She found a little coffee shop in Black Jack's Street where she nursed a fresh ground coffee, picked at a slice of carrot cake and considered her options. Her troubled mind calmed, and started to focus. Yes; she needed to get away for a while. She was not short of cash but she needed to retrieve some essentials from her room at Meadow View. She

asked the waitress for a sheet of paper and drew up a list
– clothes, underwear, night things, feminine requisites, a
large and small suitcase, travel bag and oh yes, passport,
bank statements, correspondence about her aunt's
estate . . . The list grew. She read it through. It seemed
to cover all immediate eventualities. Now to take action !

There is much park land in and around
Cirencester and Frances wandered over to an open spot
just to the north of the church, well out of earshot of any
passerby. It was now quarter to five. She selected
Sharon's number and awaited her reply.

"Ah, hello Sharon. Has he gone? . . . Good.
Look; I'm going to have to go away for a while. Can you
do something for me? . . . Tell the trustees that I've had
to attend to a family crisis and have had to go off
suddenly. Then can you go to my room and pack some
things for me and bring them here to Cirencester. Have
you a pen and paper? . . . Good. Here's my list . . ."

Frances called out the items one by one.

"Can you meet me with all this stuff at seven
o'clock at the Waitrose car park just off Sheep
Street? . . . Thanks a million."

At the appointed time the rendezvous was
accomplished. Cases and bags were transferred from
Sharon's white Vauxhall Corsa to Frances' yellow
Renault Megane.

"Thank you so much Sharon. You're a life
saver." Frances hugged Sharon.

"Where will you go Frances" asked the senior
care assistant.

"I don't know – just away from here for awhile.
I'll ring you when my plans are a bit clearer. You'll be in
charge at Meadow View for now. And don't worry.

Things will be all right". Another hug and the two women went their separate ways.

Before leaving the Waitrose car park, Frances rang her ex colleague Nancy Smythe. "Hi Nancy. It's Frances, Frances Flynn. Could I ask you a big favour? Is there any chance you could put me up for the night at your place? I'll explain all when I see you – Oh thanks – I'll see you in about half an hour." And with that she went into the supermarket to buy two bottles of Pinot Grigio and a box of Black Magic chocolates and set off for Nancy's house in Gloucester.

Nancy was a plumpish, blond, good natured woman, of about Frances' age, happily married to Harry, a thin, quiet but hard working building society officer. "Oo ! Black Magic !" exclaimed Nancy. "You remembered; they're my favourite. You know I shouldn't, but I can't resist. I'm supposed to be on a diet, but hey I could have worse weaknesses."

Frances thought of her husband and of Darren and agreed "Yes indeed you could."

The Smythe's cosy three-bed-roomed semi was in the Tuffley district of Gloucester, their youngest daughter, Emily, was already a-bed and the older girl, Sarah, now at primary school, was about to say her 'good nights'. "Up to bed with you, now and I'll tuck you in after you've brushed your teeth. Say 'good night' to Sister Frances." The child did as told and disappeared upstairs. "Harry is out at choir practice, so we have a chance to talk and catch up. Let's crack open a bottle of wine. Now, tell me what's up."

Frances told the whole long saga of her job, inheritance, marital problems, of how Brother Richard had saved her from Gerry's violent attack, of how her saviour had been disciplined and how she missed him.

She gave an update on the, apparently promising progress with Darren and then the renewed pursuit of her by Gerry, that very day.

"Cor ! You don't have your troubles to seek, do you?" sympathised Nancy.

"The fact is," confirmed Frances, "I need to put distance between myself and Gerry until I can find a way to protect myself and my birthright."

"Well, you're safe here and you're welcome to stay for a while if you need to," Nancy soothed. "I've never met Gerry, and I shouldn't say this, but some of our friends, who did, were sceptical of your choice of husband."

"Oh, don't I know that now," Frances was only too willing to confess "and thanks for the offer of sanctuary. You know, it does my heart good to see you and Harry so well settled here after the wild times we had in Liverpool."

"I'm very lucky," said Nancy. And so the conversation continued between the two old friends until Harry came home to help them finish the second bottle of wine.

That night, after a fitful start, Frances slept soundly. In the morning she joined the family for breakfast. "If you don't mind me staying one more night, I'll be off in the morning once I've had a chance to make some plans. Do you mind if I use your computer while you are at work? And I'll make the meal for tonight." This was readily agreed, a spare door key lent, information exchanged and each of the family went their various ways to work, school and nursery.

In the quiet of that happy home, Frances thought through her next move. By half past ten she had made up her mind to head for Ireland. First step: phone Finbarr to see if she could stay with him.

"Hello big brother 'mo croí'," as she lapsed into the familial Donegal brogue. "How're ye goin? . . . I'm glad to hear it . . . Oh fine and not so fine . . . I'm coming over to Dublin tomorrow. Could you be putting me up for a few days? . . . Yes . . . yes . . . no . . . I'll tell you all about it when I see you. I'll email you with my ferry times. 'Slán'."

On the Smythe's computer she checked the ferry schedules and booked herself for the following day onto the 14:30 fast Irish Ferries sailing from Holyhead to Dublin. She checked the AA Route Planner for the journey time and then emailed Finbarr with her likely arrival in the middle of the Dublin rush hour. That was all the planning necessary for the time being and with a lighter heart Frances set off on foot for down-town Gloucester to enjoy the exercise and get food for the family meal.

That evening all enjoyed a hearty evening meal of leg of lamb, gravy, mashed potatoes, sprouts and carrots followed by fruit salad. The after dinner conversation was good humoured – hilarious at times – as the two women recalled some of their outrageous student day antics, spiced at times by surprisingly dry and drol comments from Harry. Frances slept that night the sleep of the just.

In the morning (Thursday) after breakfast, Frances Flynn thanked her hosts warmly and set off for Holyhead. Her route took her north onto the M5 and then the M6 by which time it was raining hard. She was thinking about Brother Richard, without whom, who knows what would have happened to her at the hands of Gerry. She wondered what he was doing at Whitleigh, now that the bell tower was finished. Little did she realise that he was about half an hour behind her in his Transit van also heading north on the same motorway. Of course their routes deviated, as Frances branched off west by the M56 and A55 for North Wales and the port of Holyhead, while Brother Richard would continue north to Scotland.

The crossing to Dublin was uneventful and she arrived at Finbarr's house at about half past five. He had left work early to be home for her. He opened the door, put his arms round his little sister, hugged her and said: "Bail ó Dhia ort, a thaisce, agus fáilte romhat ar ais go hÉirin. Buail isteach anseo."*

---

* Loosely translated from Irish Gaelic: Bless you precious, and welcome back to Ireland. Come away inside now.

IT WAS AFTER TEN on that first night in Scotland
before Brother Richard was free to leave the police
station. Not having a mobile phone, and after finding
the body, of what he had rightly deduced was that of
Alexander Agnew, he drove to the nearby town of
Whithorn to report the incident to the local constabulary.
It was a distressing business but Brother Richard was
surprised at the very aggressive attitude of the police.
They probed into his purpose at Dalmannoch and were
sceptical of his status as a monk. It was as though he
were prime suspect in what was most certainly a murder
case. Only after a phone call to Prior John Ainslie, at
Whitleigh Priory, did the law enforcers indicate that they
were sufficiently satisfied to let him go – for the present
– but under instruction not to leave the area until further
notice.

Worn out though he was, he couldn't face the
prospect of going back to Dalmannoch in the dark to try
to find a place to sleep, bearing in mind that the
electricity supply would have been cut off. He decided
that his best prospect for the night was to sleep in the van.
Looking at his road map it was clear that the
southernmost tip of the peninsula in which Dalmannoch
and Whithorn were located was just three or four miles
away: a place called Isle of Whithorn.

Ten minutes later, he was there; past a row of
houses to a harbour and a car park at the end of the road.
Exhaustion overcame him. He cast off his shoes, spread
himself out over the driver and passenger seats and
lapsed into a deep sleep punctuated only by swirling and
unpleasant dreams that featured policemen, motorway

horror, legal conundrums and the unfathomable intentions of prior of Whitleigh.

The sun was already quite high in the eastern sky when Brother Richard woke with a start. For a few moments he wondered where he was; then he remembered. "Ouch !" Stiffly he sat up to look out at a picturesque little port. He opened the driver's door and – Ah the familiar and welcome salty smell of the sea. He stepped down and wandered along the short pier that jutted into the harbour and took in the assortment of boats lying on the mud, for it was low tide. Mostly pleasure craft, small yachts, open boats, a few inshore fishing craft, and almost all were of GRP, that is to say plastic, construction, or 'Tupperware' as his Brixham fishermen friends would have it. There was one exception – a fine lined sizable impeccably restored traditional tall masted wooden cutter – probably a hundred years old or more. Now that was a vessel with a pedigree.

Turning back the way he had come he noticed that between the village and the open sea there was a green hillock. A brisk walk up that would dispel the stiffness from the night's uncomfortable sleeping arrangement. He passed a small obviously very old roofless building; a former church possibly. At the top of the hillock there was a viewpoint and white structure in the form of a cube set up as a navigational marker.

From there, although of no great elevation, a glorious panorama opened out in all directions. To the north beyond the village and its little harbour, lay a rolling pastoral peninsula with the high Galloway hills beyond. To the east unfolded the headlands of the Galloway coast with more hills on the far horizon, presumably the fells of Cumbria. Just below him to the west ran the rocky inlet that led to the sheltered haven of Isle of Whithorn with some headland not far beyond and to the south on the expanse of open sea, the bluish hills of a large island could be discerned. An inspiring view of this kind always seemed to have an uplifting effect on Brother Richard, especially if accompanied by sea air. As he thus absorbed the wonders of creation, he was startled by a voice behind him.

"Fine view, isn't it." There stood a large pleasant looking man in sports jacket and walking boots. "Are you a local?" enquired the stranger.

"No, in fact I just arrived last night."

A conversation ensued, not dissimilar to that of the previous day with the lawyer, Robert Heron, at the Tebay service station. Educated Scots seem to have a knack of wheedling personal information from strangers without seeming to be nosey. Brother Richard was soon to discover that this was merely a natural openness and interest in a fellow human – a trait far removed from the archetypical southern English reserve of the 'respectable' classes. It transpired that the man was Ruairidh Alasdair Macdonald, a Professor at the MacPhedran Institute of Celtic Studies in Inverness, currently undertaking some research in Galloway.

He pointed out a number of the features visible from where they stood . . . "and that island on the horizon is the Isle of Man – a most interesting place.

"I'm going for breakfast now. Would you like to join me?" enquired Professor Macdonald. It was then that Brother Richard realised that he was ravenously hungry. He hadn't eaten since lunchtime the day before.

"Yes, indeed: very good idea."

The pair retraced their steps back to the village to an inn overlooking the harbour in which the professor was lodging. It was called The Steam Packet Inn, as exhibited on a large name-board wall-mounted between the ground and upper floors. The board also bore a kind of crest with crossed flags and the motto "PORUS ADRAM". Brother Richard puzzled over the Latin until he realised that it wasn't Latin at all !

"I have a room with a view of the harbour and the food is excellent."

And as regards the food he was right. On the advice of the professor, Brother Richard partook of orange juice, porridge, a smoked haddock and poached egg followed by unlimited tea, toast and marmalade and was replete.

Over breakfast Professor MacDonald explained something of the local area: that the sizeable peninsula stretching from Newton Stewart to the Isle of Whithorn, or rather to nearby Burrow Head, was known as the Machars, and that it was to this area, around 400 AD, that Saint Ninian brought Christianity to Scotland, setting up his church at Whithorn from whence he evangelised and converted the southern Picts. In fact before the Reformation, the high esteem in which Ninian was held was such that Whithorn had been a major international place of pilgrimage frequented by Scottish monarchs and other notables. The ruined building passed on the morning ramble had in fact been a chapel built around 1300 to serve the pilgrims ariving by sea on their way to St Ninian's shrine at Whithorn. Brother Richard listened with fascination to this knowlegable informant who seemed to be steeped in the history of the area.

The professor moved on to events of more recent centuries. "The Isle of Whithorn and its neighbourhood had been a haunt of smugglers, landing and transporting inland, wines, spirits and other luxuries such as tobacco and tea from the Isle of Man. Duty was negligible on the island compared with the high tax levied on the British mainland. This brisk, and at times violent, 'running trade', as it was euphamistically called, was not illegal according to Manx law but was fiercely opposed by the British Excise. In fact there is an old tower house still standing here at Isle of Whithorn that was once occupied by Sir John Ried who was Superintendent of the Coastguard charged with suppressing the trade. As you will have noticed the Isle of Whithorn is not an island, but in Sir John's day, in a sense, it was, for the spit of land connecting the village to the Machars proper flooded at high water, creating a shallow second eastern access to and from the harbour."

The professor then related a tale of those times. "Early one morning, Sir John, in command of his Revenue cutter, surprised a Manx lugger, laden with contraband. Defying the order to heave too, the lugger made a run for it in the freshening south-westerly breeze, hotly pursued by Sir John. The two vessels raced for Burrow head with the Revenue cutter gradually gaining on the Manxmen. The excisemen were relieved to see the lugger making for Isle of Whithorn, as if resigned to capture and the cutter shortened sail to follow the smuggler into the port. On arrival Sir John was astonished to find no lugger there. The intrepid Manxmen had passed through the harbour at full speed and, it being high tide, had exited by the narrow and shallow eastern channel to make their escape. When the tide had ebbed, some locals inspected the scene and found a hundred yard groove cut in the shingle made by the keel of racing smugglers. Ah yes, stirring times indeed !

Before I got carried away with smugglers tales, I mentioned Saint Ninian's mission. Would you like to tell me a little of your own mission?" the professor enquired: "You say you are here to renovate the old retreat at Dalmannoch. The name is Gaelic by the way. It means monks' meadow; as far as we know because the brothers at Whithorn pastured cattle or sheep there. I have only been there once but, of course, it was all locked up and I couldn't gain entry."

"Well that can be put right today", Brother Richard butted in. "I'm heading over there this morning. "I haven't actually been inside yet myself", at which, he explained the disturbing circumstances of the previous evening.

"A strange business Richard" sympathised the professor, "very disquieting for you. Do the police have any idea who was responsible?"

"I think they thought I was, until they phoned my prior at Whitleigh" confided the monk. "Maybe they still do. The oddest thing is; Mr. Agnew's car wasn't there at Dalmannoch. So how did he get there? He must have been taken, presumably by the murderer. I suppose that's why I must have seemed like a prime suspect. It's an awful business.

"Oh my; how distressing. I wouldn't want to intrude on your troubles", sympathised the professor.

"On the contrary" interposed Brother Richard, "After last night's experience, I'd welcome your company – just in case. Then, I guess I should go to Agnew, Douglas and McWhirter's office in Wigtown to introduce myself and give my condolences before they close for the weekend."

Professor Macdonald insisted on paying for both breakfasts, then suggested: "Whithorn is on our way.

Why don't we stop there for an hour or so to look at the remains of the old priory and what the recent archaeological digs have come up with." With that, each man went to his respective vehicle, in the professor's case an elderly dark green Volvo V70 Estate, even older than the Transit van, and they set off in convoy on the short distance to Whithorn.

BROTHER RICHARD was captivated by the whole atmosphere of the quaint little Royal Burgh of Whithorn with its wide medieval main street narrowing at each end, the ecclesiastical remains, ancient cross slabs and much more, not least because he was privileged to have an expert guide at hand. He could have stayed for hours but Dalmannoch awaited.

The pair continued in convoy with Brother Richard's van in the lead until they turned up Dalmannoch's narrow curved drive and through the patch of woodland. As they approached the neat assemblage of buildings they were confronted by a tall police sergeant, clad in a high visibility yellow coat, and holding up his hand to stop them. Brother Richard lowered his side window and was told:

"I'm afraid ye canna come onie further sir. This is a crime scene." Brother Richard pondered for a few seconds about the previous night's officious interrogation and decided with a spark of mischief to make a stand. "But this is my home."

"Ye'r home sir?" said the policeman with a measure of puzzlement, "Hoo lang hae ye lived here?"

"That's the trouble," explained the monk, "I haven't."

"Ye havna sir? "Whit dae ye mean ye havna?"

"Well I arrived yesterday afternoon to find the body of Mr. Agnew on – er – my doorstep – and – when I reported this at the Whithorn Police Station, you chaps kept me so long with questions that it was dark, so I had to sleep in my van."

By this point the professor had got out of his car to join the conversation. "What's the problem Richard?"

The policeman repeated his mantra: "This is a crime scene. You canna come onie further."

The group was now joined by another obviously more senior police officer. "Whit's going on George." The sergeant explained the gist of the exchange and Brother Richard emerged from the driver's seat to stand beside the professor. The senior policeman, switching from Broad Scots to what grammarians term Scottish Standard English, addressed Brother Richard.

"Good morning sir. You are, I believe, Mr. Richard Wells who reported the murder?"

"<u>Brother</u> Richard Wells – yes I am," corrected the monk.

"I'm D.I. Morrison. I'm in charge of this murder investigation and this is a crime scene. I'm sorry Mr. – em – Brother Wells, but I can't let you in until we have carried out our forensic investigation."

In confirmation of this, two men in white suits appeared from behind a police van stationed where Brother Richard had parked the previous afternoon.

With a growing sense of foreboding, Brother Richard asked; "When will you be finished?"

"I can't say at the moment sir." Inspector Morrison was polite but firm. "My men are about to force entry to the building."

"Force entry?" queried Brother Richard. Why not use a key?"

"Because we have been unable to locate a key sir" said the inspector with a hint of impatience. "Now I must ask you to leave."

"But I have a key" pronounced the monk, with poorly concealed triumph. He rummaged for the envelope and pulled out a pair of keys. Tied to the smaller of the two was a buff luggage label upon which were written the words:

DALMANNOCH
FRONT DOOR

"Ah – I see." The inspector seemed to lighten up a little. "If I may borrow it please; it will be returned to you directly."

Brother Richard stiffened. "You are welcome to use it of course; these are the only keys I have. I wish to be as helpful as possible but I'll need them to get into the building. This is now my place of residence. I have already spent one uncomfortable night sleeping in my van. I'd rather not spend another." Brother Richard continued in frustration: "I'm a monk. I have been sent here from Whitleigh Priory, more than 400 miles away in the south west of England. I am tasked with renovating this building. I discovered the murdered body of Mr. Agnew here yesterday afternoon. I reported this to the police and for my pains was interrogated as though I had committed the crime myself. I'm a man of God, or try to be. I don't murder people. I have no money of my own and I have been instructed by your colleagues not to leave the area. Where am I supposed to rest my head while your people poke about indefinitely?"

The professor had been listening to the on-going dialogue. He now sought to mediate: "Inspector, we appreciate that the police have a job to do here and that procedures have to be followed, but from what I understand you have been pretty hard on my friend. It would be appreciated if he could get access as soon as reasonably possible so that he can settle in and get on with his duties."

"And who are you?" enquired the inspector.

The professor stifled a very strong urge to express the Scots repost "I'm fine, hoo's yersel'" and instead answered with a factual "My name is Ruairidh Alasdair Macdonald."

"Well Mr. Macdonald"

"Professor Macdonald" corrected the academic.

"Professor Macdonald, the forensic investigation will take as long as it takes but I will ensure that Brother Wells can enter his residence as soon as we are able to allow that."

Turning back to Brother Richard, Inspector Morrison smiled a patient smile and held out his hand "Now sir, the key please. I will get it back to you as soon as I can." Brother Richard obeyed and passed over the pair of keys. "Now where can I find you to return them?"

"As I have tried to explain; that's the problem. I have no where to stay. And before you ask, I have no mobile phone."

All the while, unnoticed by the group, a small thin man in brown leather zipper jacket, beige slacks and green suede desert boots was taking in the whole exchange. He introduced himself as John Shaw, but was known throughout Galloway as Jock the Shock on account of the sensational character of his writing. Notebook and recording device in hand, the reporter asked Brother Richard what he felt about the police handling of the case.

"Well I – em – it's been upsetting. I was shocked to find Mr. Agnew's – er – body here – and . . ."

The journalist persisted "But the police. I understand that their methods have been heavy handed."

At this Inspector Morrison intervened. "That's enough Jock. Our enquiries are at an early stage. The Police will make a full statement to the press in due course."

Professor Macdonald took Brother Richard's elbow. "Look Richard, I think we should go now. We can call for the keys later."

The inspector nodded courteously: "Thank you gentlemen; I can assure you that we will be as quick as we can, subject to us completing our forensic search. You will be able to pick up the keys at Wigtown Police Station when we have finished"

As he turned to re-board the Transit van, an inspired thought occurred to the ever practical Brother Richard. "Oh – one thing Inspector Morrison: it has occurred to me that the building will be in complete darkness. There will be no power connection and the windows are boarded up. It will help your men and it would be a favour to me if you were to remove the shuttering. But leave it in a pile. It may come in useful."

The inspector smiled. He was developing a sneaking admiration for this out of the ordinary monk. "You've got a deal." He added: "I hope you find somewhere to stay tonight. Why don't you try Father McGuire at St Aidan's?"

Ruairidh Macdonald consulted his watch. It was quarter past twelve. "Look; you have to go to Wigtown to see the solicitors and I have to go there too to pick up a manuscript that has been reserved for me, then I'm off to Newton Stewart to meet some contacts at half past two. Why don't we have a bite of lunch there, then we can go our separate ways. And later, if you like, we could meet up to compare notes"

"Sounds good to me" agreed Brother Richard.

A PARKING PLACE for van and Volvo was easily found on Wigtown's South Main Street. The two men alighted from their respective vehicles.

"Wigtown's an unusual place" proclaimed the professor.

Exasperated, Brother Richard burst out: "Unusual ?! – Unusual ?! I've not been in Scotland twenty four hours and I've had nothing but 'unusual' episodes ! – Murder; fearful interrogation; a fitful uncomfortable night; meeting a walking historical encyclopaedia; an inquisitive hack; banned by the police from my new home, God help me – and – and – this warm sunny weather has challenged all my preconceived notions of the Scottish climate. If I have any more 'unusuals' I think I'll – I'll . . ."

"Burst ?" suggested the professor, laughing. "With luck, Wigtown won't have that effect. What's unusual about this little old county town and royal burgh is that it's hotchin with second-hand book shops."

"Hotchin ?" queried Brother Richard. "Sorry Richard – a Scots word. It means 'abounding in'; 'infested with'. Wigtown is Scotland's National Book Town."

Amused by this outburst, the professor led Brother Richard round a corner to a small café, Café Rendezvous, where a free table was found and over a light lunch the pair reviewed the morning's events.

"I have to agree with you Richard," confessed the professor, "this morning has been 'unusual' for me too. Pity we couldn't get into Dalmannoch though. Maybe the police will be finished tomorrow if you're still up for showing me round."

Brother Richard was quick to respond: "Oh, as I said, I'd very much welcome that Ruairidh. If it's all right with you we could call again tomorrow afternoon to see if the coast's clear."

"Let's hope so," the professor agreed. "I have to be off back to Inverness on Sunday. It's end of term at the University so there is much to do there."

The monk felt some disappointment that his new found companion would be departing so soon. He was relieved, however, that the professor would be around for another day at least.

After they had eaten, (Brother Richard paid the, fortunately modest, bill) each went his separate way, having agreed to meet up again at the same café for lunch the following day. The professor set off to one of the many antiquarian bookshops in Wigtown to negotiate the purchase of a rare manuscript on one of the old Galloway families.

Brother Richard made his own way to the chambers of the legal firm Agnew, Douglas and McWhirter. He was directed to an open doorway in North Main Street adjacent to another bookshop. A flight of stairs led to a first floor landing and a series of glass panelled doors, one of which was labelled 'Reception'. He entered to find, in one corner a series of chairs round a coffee table laden with out-of-date magazines, and in the opposite corner, a bespectacled somewhat severe looking middle-aged woman behind a desk. A small metal sign on the desk displayed the name: 'E MacDowall'.

"Good afternoon – em – Mrs. MacDowell. My name is Richard Wells – Brother Richard. It was I who found your Mr Agnew's – em – Mr Agnew. I'm most terribly sorry. I was supposed to have met him at Dalmannoch, but then this tragic . . ."

"Miss MacDowell" emphasised the receptionist. "So you are the monk who was to meet Mr. Agnew . . ."

Both parties were finding it difficult to find words to communicate effectively. After a pause Brother Richard spoke.

"For the present, I just wanted to offer my sincere condolences to Mr. Agnew's colleagues. And I'm sorry to bring this up at this difficult time, but in due course, when it's suitable, I also need to speak to someone in the firm about the Dalmannoch Trust and the matters that Mr. Agnew and I had planned to discuss."

"This is not a good time for us." Miss MacDowell stated firmly. "Everyone is very upset. We have spent much of the morning trying to help the police. I'll pass your condolences on to the partners. Now if you wouldn't mind calling back next week, we could arrange for an appointment."

Brother Richard sympathised, "I quite understand – a very distressing time for you. I'll call back early next week. I'd be obliged if you'd let me know of the funeral arrangements once they have been set. Although I never met Mr. Agnew alive, I'd like to pay my respects."

As he made to leave the reception room, a young red-headed woman with a file under her arm entered hurriedly and in something of a fluster:

"Oh, Betty, could you . . ."

Miss MacDowell interrupted: "This is Brother Richard Wells who found Mr. Agnew yesterday. He was just leaving. I've told him to come back next week"

"Ah, Brother Richard." The red-headed woman held out her hand. "I'm Catriona Macarthur. I'm afraid we're at sixes and sevens today. It's all been too much. But Mr. Agnew's death must have been as much of a shock to you as it has been for us. Can I help at all?"

"Well, I wouldn't mind a quick word, if you have a few minutes." Brother Richard was relieved at the more positive attitude of the new arrival. Miss MacDowell, her authority undermined, looked daggers at both of them.

"I can give you five minutes just now. Come through to my office." Brother Richard followed Catriona Macarthur to a small room at the back of the building.

The young lawyer, pushing her luxuriant red locks from her face, gestured Brother Richard to sit, then sat herself behind a desk that took up most of the room. "I'm fairly new here and mainly do conveyancing but Alec – Mr. Agnew that is – told me, in the passing, that he was scheduled to meet you yesterday. I thought it strange though that a Mr. Arbuckle, an architect I believe, called to take him to Dalmannoch."

"Mr. Arbuckle? – Jamie Arbuckle?" Brother Richard was flabbergasted. "But why should Jamie . . . I don't understand . . . He wasn't to come until after I had cleaned the place up a bit. This whole business is very troubling."

"Yes it is for us too," agreed Catriona Macarthur, we were all very fond of Alec. He has no family here. His wife died some four years ago and his only sister lives in Australia."

Brother Richard sought to change tack. "I know you are all very distressed, as am I, Ms Macarthur, and very busy, but can I ask a couple of smallish things for just now?"

Catriona Macarthur assented.

58

"Well firstly, it was my intention to sleep at Dalmannoch but it is out of bounds to me until the police have finished their forensic investigation there. Meantime I have nowhere to stay. The inspector suggested I try Father McGuire at St Aidan's. Could someone here put me in touch with him by phone?"

Again Catriona Macarthur agreed that this was possible.

"And secondly, could someone from the firm arrange for the power to be put on so that I can have light and use power tools?"

"Yes I'm sure that can be arranged. I will need to see which of the partners will be handling the Dalmannoch Trust from now on. You see trusts were Alec's specialty. If you would call back early next week we can start to fix things up."

The young lawyer then apologetically ushered Brother Richard back to reception, asked the redoubtable Miss MacDowell to make the telephone connection with Father McGuire and disappeared from whence she had come.

* * *

"Father McGuire? . . . Brother Richard Wells here from Whitleigh Priory . . . yes, Whitleigh in the Cotswolds . . . Oh yes, indeed. The thing is Father McGuire, I'm in the Machars area just now and my accommodation arrangements have fallen through. I wondered if it would be possible to stay with you for a couple of nights until I get fixed up. . . It would? . . . Oh, I'm very much obliged. . . Now how do I get to St Aidan's?"

Brother Richard signalled for pen and paper, and wrote down the key directions and turnings of the route to St Aidan's, thanked Father McGuire and hung up. "Thank you Miss MacDowell, you have been very helpful."

"You are very welcome Brother Richard" and for the first time Miss MacDowell broke into a smile. "You may call me Betty; everyone else does."

As Brother Richard descended the stairway, he felt he had made a significant breakthrough; not so much in finding lodgings for the night, but in eliciting a smile from formidable Miss MacDowell.

FATHER TOM MCGUIRE, smiling and ruddy of complexion, was affable and welcoming. Brother Richard explained the circumstances of the previous twenty four hours after which the priest showed his guest to one of St Aidan's spare bedrooms suggesting that an afternoon nap might be beneficial. Brother Richard then realised that he was dog tired and took advantage of this offer. He slept luxuriantly in the comfort of a soft bed for two and a half hours. On wakening he found it was almost time for the evening meal. Before eating he sought and was granted the use of Father McGuire's telephone to make contact with Prior John Ainslie.

Since the previous night's call by the police, the prior had been decidedly apprehensive as to what had been going on at Dalmannoch. The police had not been at all forthcoming with information. The junior monk again described the sequence of events to the considerable astonishment of Prior John.

"I have to say Richard; I am shocked by this extraordinary turn of events. Are you yourself all right?"

Brother Richard almost blushed at the, normally strict and aloof, prior's concern. "Yes, yes, I'm alright . . . a bit shaken but I can cope with the job ahead." And strangely, he did feel up for the fray, despite, or maybe even because of, the circumstances. Brother Richard agreed to keep in touch regarding developments at Dalmannoch.

The meal prepared by Father McGuire's housekeeper was hearty and appetising. It was washed down by good claret followed by Port and a relaxing evening was enjoyed by them both.

* * *

Next day was Saturday. Father McGuire was not an early riser, especially on Saturdays, but in due course after breakfast was prepared and eaten, the priest urged:

"You'll stay another night at least and you can help me with Mass on Sunday."

Brother Richard concurred, and then made his excuses to head back to Wigtown. It was almost eleven o' clock and in the free hour and a half before the lunchtime rendezvous with the professor; he inspected a number of Wigtown's bookshops and was impressed by their variety. In the course of his perambulations, he called at Wigtown Police Station to enquire about the keys to Dalmannoch to be told that the forensic investigation had just been completed and he was presented with the said implements.

At the appointed time of twelve thirty, he made for the café and there, already seated, was Ruairidh Macdonald. The pair shook hands and monk joined professor at the table.

"So how did you get on at the solicitors?"

Brother Richard described the experience and his evening with Father McGuire, adding: "And yourself? Successful negotiations?"

"Indeed yes. I'm very happy with my manuscript, and will be examining it as soon as I can find time, although I probably paid more than I should. Two of my contacts in Newton Stewart were particularly edifying and, funnily enough, they were very interested to hear about Dalmannoch. They may be of some help to you."

Lunch at the Café Rendezvous was a quick and simple affair. When it was over, the two vehicle convoy set off for Dalmannoch. Both vehicles were drawn up side by side outside the chapel and this time, there was no police presence. The two men made their way towards the front door of the accommodation building.

The main building was stone, compact and built of two stories, having something of the appearance of a Victorian shooting lodge but with more than usual architectural panache, being a rather fine example of the arts-and-crafts style. There was a carved coat of arms set in a stone panel on the face of a sort of square tower above the main door. The tower was surmounted by a rusty weather vane askew to the perpendicular.

Brother Richard turned the key in the lock and pushed the front door. It opened with a creak and the pair made their way through a vestibule and into a panelled hallway with a curved stairway leading to the upper floor. A musty damp smell permeated the building and a layer of dust covered the floor and other horizontal surfaces. A mouse scuttered across the floor and disappeared through a crack in a skirting board.

To the right of the hall, a door led to what seemed like a large lounge or common room furnished with a few tired looking arm chairs and settees. As they entered, Brother Richard froze as he felt something brush across his face – a well developed web and a very large spider scuttling for cover. Behind the lounge was a lavatory and what must have been a library, judging by the wall shelving empty save for a few dusty books and papers. Back to the hall and on the left another door led to some kind of reception room with a desk and a few upright chairs, beyond which was a large empty dining room. To the back of the building was a wing with lavatory, kitchen, washhouse. An inspection of the upstairs area revealed a number of mainly empty rooms presumably bedrooms and dormitories together with closets, two bathrooms and rooms connected with the one-time management of the retreat.

"The first task here will be to give it a good thorough clean and airing, but," suggested Brother Richard; "what do you say, Ruairidh, we have a look at the chapel now?"

"You bet" said the professor. "I'd love to. I've heard it's worth seeing. Let's do that.

So, monk and professor made their way outside again to the pretty little detached stone built chapel which was set at an angle to the main building. The larger key, labelled 'CHAPEL', was now produced, placed in the keyhole and turned without too much difficulty. The heavy oak chapel door, studded with rusty ironwork groaned a little as it was pushed open. The two men passed through a tiled lobby and into the chapel proper.

"Wow !" exclaimed Professor Macdonald.

"Wow !" echoed Brother Richard.

What they beheld was a masterpiece of Victorian gothic splendour worthy of Augustus Pugin at his best – and yet somehow more magical, more free form and natural than the work of that renowned neo-Gothic architect. The white interior walls were patterned with intricate red and green Celtic knot work. The ceiling was dark blue spattered with silver stars. The high altar was a glorious confection of white marble and gilt work and the late morning sun streamed through the stained glass of the south wall to infuse the space with a bright multi-coloured light.

Brother Richard made the sign of the cross and walked to the high altar. There he knelt in silent prayer. The professor stood in respectful silence, and although a more or less lapsed Presbyterian, was equally overcome by the emotional and spiritual power of this extraordinary interior – its effect enhanced by the contrasting shabbiness of the previously visited neighbouring building. At length the two men looked at each other.

"This is very special. I've never seen anything like it." The professor spoke almost in a whisper.

Brother Richard nodded, speechless. As Professor Macdonald started to take in the complex elements of design and symbolism, he gave voice to his thoughts.

"The whole assemblage is very Catholic, but – yet – very Celtic. See the knot-work interlaced with oak leaves – and there – shield knots representing the four elements of earth, air, fire and water, of old used for warding and protection. And there a solar cross which combines a cross with a ring, representing the sun – developed as the Celtic cross, a well known symbol of Celtic Christianity, although it has older, pre-Christian origins. Celtic crosses are thought to have been taken from the early Coptic Church and to have been introduced to Ireland, by Saint Patrick when converting the Pagan Irish, and subsequently taken to Scotland. Then that there is a cross of St Brigid. Brigid, Bride or Brìd was a contemporary of Patrick and regarded as Mary of the Gaels. She was named after the powerful Pagan goddesse of healing, inspiration, craftsmanship, beef, flowers, corn, and poetry, and her festival was 1st February or Imbolc which marked the beginning of spring."

As the professor's eyes scanned the walls and ceiling he identified more and more elements of the chapel's interior decoration.

"That head there is a Green Man, another ancient symbol. He represents spring and summer re-enacting the cycle of death and resurrection, the ebb and flow of life and creativity – quite common in medieval churches but very unusual in Scottish buildings of Victorian origin. And then those little marks on the frieze are the signs of the zodiac, located, it would seem, 30° apart according to their longitudinal position. And that seven-pointed star – that is an Elven Star. The Elven Star, or Faerie Star, is representative of the seven stars of the Pleiades. Seven is of course a sacred number in many magical traditions – it is connected with the seven pillars of wisdom and the seven days of the week. Richard, what we have here is an amalgam of the Catholic, the Celtic – and the Pagan !"

Brother Richard was bowled over by this revelation. "Surely a Catholic place of worship would have nothing to do with Paganism."

"Well, these things may not be quite as incompatible as you might think – especially in this part of the world. You see Saint Ninian and the other early Celtic saints who evangelised here had to persuade a devoutly Pagan people to accept the precepts of Christianity. To achieve that, they brokered a melding of the Christian and the Pagan. Thus Christmas and Easter and other Christian festivals were adapted from the Pagan seasonal rites. The halo on holy pictures is an adaptation of the Pagan sun cult – as is the Celtic cross. However, I have never before seen quite such an explicit juxtaposition of these traditions in a Christian chapel. It's quite extraordinary."

"There's another thing. You say this place has been shut up for years; yet it's strangely clean and dust free." Brother Richard bent down to pick up a slip of paper that he noticed under the corner of a front pew. It was a bus ticket. It was dated 1st May – May Day, just three weeks old.

"Someone has been using the chapel. Mmm – the question is," speculated Brother Richard: "who? And why?"

S UNDAY was wet and windy but in many ways a relief from the turmoil of the previous few days. Brother Richard acted as aide-de-camp to Father Tom McGuire with Mass at St Aidan's and in general helping with his relatively undemanding clerical responsibilities. While Father Tom was a genial host, Brother Richard found the rich meals served at St Aidan's, coupled with copious alcoholic refreshment, hard on his digestion. Furthermore, Father Tom was a chain smoker and a passionate and voluble devotee of the Glasgow Celtic Football Club, neither of which held much attraction for the good father's guest. In view of all this, Brother Richard, while eternally grateful for his host's benevolence in his hour of need, decided to move out of St Aidan's on the Monday morning, to buy some provisions and settle in at Dalmannoch.

On arrival, after a further tour of the accommodation building, opening such windows as he could, to air the building, it was clear that the next priority was cleaning the place. The van had been partially unloaded into the reception room on Saturday, with the help of Professor Macdonald prior to his departure. Brother Richard transferred the remainder of the van's payload into that space then set to brushing out and washing down the walls of the hallway and common room, with the aim of making the latter his living and sleeping area for the immediate future. Such was the accumulation of dust, cobwebs and other detritus that this task took up the rest of that Monday.

As he pressed on with this somewhat menial work, he considered what had happened since he had left

Whitleigh Priory. So much had transpired that it seemed like weeks ago. In fact only four nights had passed and he was now in his fifth day since that fateful drive north. The murder of Alexander Agnew was undoubtedly the pivotal and most shocking event which had derailed the undertaking Prior John had given him, temporarily at least. He thought too of the assortment of people he had come across over those few days.

There was the Solicitor Robert Heron whom he had met at Tebay who had spoken so warmly of Alexander Agnew, or AA as he called him. Had he heard of the murder? No doubt the word will have travelled round such a tight knit rural community. Then there was that harrowing police interview, compensated to some extent by the more courteous approach of Detective Inspector Morrison. It was Professor Ruairidh Macdonald, however, who eased the trauma. Brother Richard felt he had found a new friend and developed a special bond with this erudite but good-humoured academic. He hoped they would meet again when the professor's end-of-term academic chores were concluded.

As he wiped down the panelled walls of the hallway, he was amused to remember his rather brief encounter at Agnew, Douglas and McWhirter of how the young solicitor with luxuriant red hair, Catriona Macarthur, was able to get the fearsome Miss MacDowell to make contact with Father Tom and how he was able in the end to get 'Betty' to smile. He thought Cartiona Macarthur perhaps a little scatty and wondered if she had in fact made contact with the electricity company to re-connect the power supply. Fortunately he had candles and paraffin Tilley lamp and Primus stove to give him illumination and permit basic kettle boiling and cooking in the meantime. One bonus of nature as far as illumination was concerned was that, at this time of year in Scotland, it does not get dark till late. But electricity would be required if he was to do any serious work on the building and he made a mental note to visit the solicitors the following day to chase things up and to ascertain the rôle of the Dalmannoch trust, not least in releasing funds to enable remedial works to progress.

One of the most puzzling things about his visit to the solicitors was the throw away line by Catriona Macarthur about Jamie Arbuckle. Why on earth had Jamie picked up Alexander Agnew to take him to Dalmannoch? It seemed inconceivable that Jamie had murdered the lawyer. What motive could he have? In any case it just seemed so out of character. He thought of Jamie's sure guiding hand in the design and construction of the bell tower at Whitleigh and his passion for traditional design and materials, albeit aided by modern technology. Yes sometimes he had been tetchy, short tempered even, when things went wrong or materials were sub-standard, but murder? The fact was: Brother Richard had formed a good relationship with Jamie Arbuckle. Perhaps something had pushed the architect over the edge, he had seemed a bit stressed of late, yet it was just so difficult to believe that he could have resorted to murder.

That night he lit a fire of scrap wood in the common room, made up his camp bed, cooked a plain vegetarian meal on the Primus, washed down by a cup of tea and brought to mind the more measured pace of life at Whitleigh. He felt quite relaxed after the day's exertions and had regained a degree of equilibrium. As he crawled into his sleeping bag he recalled his visits to Meadow View. He thought about Tom Bayliss and his wayward grandson, but most of all he thought about

Sister Frances. Where was she? What was she doing? Was she all right?

* * *

Next morning was grey and threatening rain. Brother Richard rose early and, after boiling water for a shave and cursory cold wash in a still grimy bathroom, he made his way to the chapel to contemplate his God with whom, notwithstanding his monastic training, he had an as yet uneasy relationship. The chapel had, inexplicably, both a comforting and troubling effect.

Breakfast followed. Father Tom's housekeeper had shown Brother Richard the secret of the Scottish method of making and eating porridge – absolutely no sugar; a little salt and then a cup of cold milk to accompany it. Oat meal had been purchased the previous day to initiate this wholesome breakfast practice that had fortified generations of hardy Scots in setting out to build an empire. Thus fortified, Brother Richard drove to Wigtown and made for the chambers of Agnew, Douglas and McWhirter.

Brother Richard risked a: "good morning Betty", to receive in return a smile and a:

"Good morning Brother Richard". Progress indeed.

"Would it be possible for me to make an appointment to see someone who can help me with the Dalmannoch Trust?"

"Yes of course", verified Betty, "Ms Macarthur has been expecting you. I believe she is free just now, but just let me check."

Betty lifted the phone and, on enquiring, was able to confirm that Ms Macarthur was indeed free to see the brother.

"Ah yes, good morning Brother Richard. I have been assigned your case – that is the Dalmannoch Trust. I'm afraid I still have a bit of catching up to do but I have skimmed the file and read through the original trust deed, so I should be able to deal with some of your immediate requirements."

Brother Richard was pleasantly surprised that this previously harassed young woman seemed to have brought matters under some kind of control.

He opened negotiations with: "Firstly let me thank the firm for finding me lodgings with Father McGuire while Dalmannoch was out of bounds. I am now, however, ensconced at Dalmannoch and have made a start in cleaning the place up. But you will understand that my first requirement is for electricity. Have you been able to make progress on that front?"

"Yes I have", confirmed the lawyer. "I phoned Scotia Energy on Friday just after you called and have put that in train. I followed it up yesterday and have forwarded the trust's bank details with a formal instruction to proceed. I believe someone should turn up tomorrow to check the meter and get the power switched on."

Once again Brother Richard was impressed and thanked Ms. Macarthur for her promptness.

He continued, "The other key requirement is money. If we are to get Dalmannoch into saleable condition, I will need access to funds to purchase materials and for other expenses."

"Again, that should present no great difficulties", confirmed Ms. Macarthur, "The trust still has a fairly substantial balance with the Royal Caledonian Bank here in Wigtown and I will arrange for accounts to be opened at such builders' merchants as you are likely to use and you can make personal impresses for reasonable minor expenses."

"Well, I can but thank you for you efficiency Ms. Macarthur. I shall try to be as economical as I can with my renovations. Perhaps we can have another meeting in a week or two's time to work out a way forward regarding the future of Dalmannoch and its possible sale."

Catriona Macarthur agreed that this was appropriate and that she required more time to research the background to the trust and in particular Alexander Agnew's recent involvement.

Catriona Macarthur added: "By the way, I see you have made the Sunday papers, or at least the *Sunday Sketch*, if you can call that scurrilous rag a newspaper."

With that Brother Richard departed from the premises of Agnew, Douglas and McWhirter, and, in passing reception, eliciting another smile and a "Good day Brother Richard" from Betty.

B ACK AT DALMANNOCH, more sweeping and washing down as a growing pile of rubbish built up on the gravel outside the front door. Catriona Macarthur had told him that the Council recycling centre was to be found not far from Dalmannoch and she gave him directions as to how to find it. By midday, such was the size of the pile that a visit to this facility had become necessary and after loading the van, he set off. Getting rid of unwanted material was one thing, but Brother Richard discovered that the recycling centre was a treasure trove of all sorts of useful items. Once the van was unloaded, he "rescued" two very serviceable chairs, a coffee table and a large bookcase – a little scruffy perhaps, but they would polish up quite nicely.

It was mid afternoon, while cleaning out one of the upstairs bathrooms, that the sound of a car drawing up outside, followed by the clunk of a door, attracted Brother Richard's attention. He went downstairs to investigate. There, standing outside the open front door, surveying the exterior of the building, was Jamie Arbuckle.

"Jamie ! What on earth !"

"Well you might say 'what on earth' Richard", said Jamie Arbuckle. "You'll not believe what I've been through over the last couple of days."

"You'd better come inside. I'll put the kettle on." Brother Richard led Jamie into the now much cleaner if still somewhat shabby common room, pumped and lit the Primus propped up on the newly acquired coffee table, and on it, placed the kettle.

"I don't like to be critical Richard, but it isn't really safe to be using a paraffin stove in a room like this. Have you not got a kitchen?" Thus spoke the architect.

The monk countered, "Yes but you should see the state of it. Listen, I'll show you round after we've had tea, and OK, I promise, after this I'll use the kitchen, but it'll need a good clean up. But before we do anything tell me what's been going on. After that, I'll tell you about my adventures."

Jamie Arbuckle started his tale.

"Well, I planned to take a long weekend off to stay with my uncle in Moffat and enjoy a bit of golf. I left the office in Leith, Edinburgh that is, quite early on Thursday morning to visit a job in Biggar. A client there is renovating an Edwardian villa and we are trying to make it as 'carbon free' as possible without spoiling its essential character. There are a few problems with rot, but the builder and I have worked out a course of action. He's a fairly competent guy, but I have to keep an eye on him. Anyway, I was finished there by about one o' clock and was free at last. My long weekend had started, so I went to the Cross Keys in the High Street by Cadger's Bridge for a bite of lunch.

It must have been about two when I left the Cross Keys, so I headed towards Moffat. It was a glorious day and I decided to park the car and to walk into the Devil's Beef Tub. It's a deep, hollow in the hills just a few miles north of Moffat. It was used in the old days by the Border Rievers to hide rustled cattle. It's quite spectacular. I hadn't been there since I was a bairn. Then I climbed Great Hill and the views were spectacular, so clear and crisp was the day. It was great just to be free of the office and clients. It must have been nearly six o' clock by the time I got back to the car and I headed straight to Moffat and Uncle Mata's house. His welcome is always the same: 'Come awa ben ma laddie. Ye'll be needin yer tea', which indeed I was. I guess I'm Uncle Mata's favourite and we yarned that evening until late. Most of Saturday and Sunday was spent on the golf course. You know, Moffat Golf Club's course was designed by the legendary Ben Sayers and commands amazing views in all directions. It's regarded as one of the best inland courses in the country. The ninth hole is extraordinary. It has a scary par-3, on rising ground that ends in a towering rock face with the green just over the top – great golfing altogether."

As with football, Brother Richard had little interest in golf, but he nodded encouragingly and as the kettle was boiling, interrupted Jamie's flow by pouring the hot water over the tea-bags placed in a pair of mugs and asked. "Milk ? Sugar ?"

"Just milk thanks. So all in all," continued Jamie, sipping his tea, "it was the most agreeable weekend I've had for ages. I went back to the office full of beans yesterday morning and then all Hell broke loose."

"I got there about ten o' clock. The police were interrogating those of my colleagues and contacts that they had been unable to locate during the weekend, as to my whereabouts. When I wandered in, happy as you like, they pounced on me and bundled me into a police car. I was taken first to Leith Police Station in Queen Charlotte Street. They bombarded me with questions about what I was up to on Thursday and what involvement I had with Dalmannoch and Teddy North and how well I knew Alexander Agnew. Well I had never met Alexander Agnew or Teddy North and of course I only knew about Dalmannoch from what the prior at Whitleigh had mentioned. They didn't believe me. It was then, Richard that I realised that I was suspected of murder. They whisked me off to Dumfries where I spent the night in a cell. This morning they arranged an identity parade, but the old biddy that is supposed to have seen the murderer, didn't pick me out. Well naturally – it wasn't me. She seemed quite sure of herself and didn't pick any of those in the line up. It was scary though, I can tell you Richard. Apparently the lawyer, who was killed, was picked up by an architect or someone calling himself Mr. Arbuckle just before his body was found."

"The main problem I had was that I had no alibi for the time the murder took place. I was, as I said, on my own at the Devil's Beef Tub. Thank God, around the same time as the identity parade, it seems they found a farmer, a Mr Kirkpatrick, who saw me come down off the Great Hill and head for my car. Thank God too for his powers of observation. He remembered the car and the 'JAM' number plate. I know everyone thinks its pretentious style over substance, but just as well I have that red Alfa Romeo Spider Convertible and a 'cherished number'. I guess in this instance it saved my bacon. Anyway the police let me go. I phoned the office to let them know everything was OK. After that I decided to come over to Dalmannoch to see what all the fuss was about."

"Well, well, Jamie. You've certainly been through the mill", commiserated Brother Richard.

"Mind you, so have I. I'm sure they thought I was a murder suspect too" and he described the chain of events since finding the body.

"But tell me who is Teddy North? That's a new one on me."

"Ah," explained Jamie, "Teddy or Edward North is a property developer – a bit dodgy by all accounts.

Some call him 'Neddy North'. I've never met him. He made millions on poorly designed and over priced housing developments, retail parks and that sort of thing, but they say he overstretched himself and was caught out by the financial crisis. Put it this way; I wouldn't want to touch him with the proverbial barge pole."

Stories exchanged and tea consumed, Brother Richard changed the subject. "How do you fancy a look round Dalmannoch now that you're here?"

"I'd love to", confirmed the architect and Brother Richard took proprietarily pride in acting as guide to the main building. Jamie poked about as architects do and concluded:

"This place has possibilities. It's well built, it has interesting architectural detailing and isn't in bad nick – considering."

"Wait till you see the chapel," the monk declared with a hint of smugness, and both men made there way thence.

"Jeepers ! amazing !" was exactly the reaction Brother Richard expected of Jamie and was not disappointed. He then pointed out the eclectic mix and significance of Catholic, Celtic and Pagan symbolism as previously explained by Professor Macdonald.

"This place must be looked after. It's a gem."

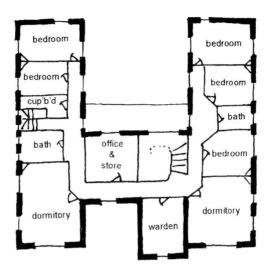

Dalmannoch upper floor plan

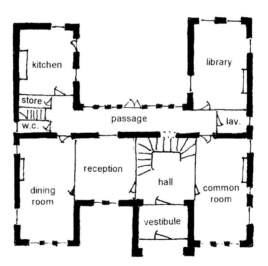

Dalmannoch Ground Floor Plan

79

W HILE BROTHER RICHARD was coming to terms with the diverse issues thrown up by Dalmannoch, Frances Flynn was coming to terms with life as a fugitive. Since she had arrived in Dublin she felt safe with the Irish Sea between herself and Gerry. Besides; she had not had quality time with her brother Finbarr for longer than she cared to think.

Finbarr was a well-doing accountant with a firm specialising in company insolvencies and liquidations. Business had been brisk since the financial crisis had hit Ireland and he lived in comfort, with his long standing girl friend Imelda, in a four bed detached house in the prosperous northern coastal Dublin dormitory village of Portmarnock.

"Sure you can stay here as long as you want." Frances was grateful for Finbarr's generous offer but knew it would be unfair on Imelda to outstay her welcome. She would be off again, in a few days, she knew not where. Meantime, Finbarr and she reminisced about their childhood, about their late father, Sean McGarrigle, how their mother was getting along and about the world – a special time for both of them.

A few days after she arrived in Dublin, Finbarr, on his way to work, dropped Frances off in the city. She had wanted to enjoy some of the sights and sounds of Ireland's vibrant capital. She wandered along College Green passed Trinity College and up Grafton Street past the bronze statue of Molly Malone and her wheelbarrow, known irreverently to Dubliners as 'The Tart with the Cart'. The pedestrianised southern section of Grafton Street is, or was, said to be the fifth most expensive main shopping street in the world, famed also for its cafés and pubs. Frances lapped up the buskers, the familiar sights, smells and sounds and the humour of the Dublin 'craic'. This pleasant perambulation proceeded on up to St Steven's Green with its lakes and ducks and then she turned back down Kildare Street past the National Library to the National Gallery of Ireland.

Frances' interest in art had been encouraged by her late Aunt Mary. As a consequence, when in Dublin, she tried to make a point of visiting the National Gallery with its coverage of all the major Continental schools from the 14th century and most of all its comprehensive collection of Irish artists including her favourite, Jack B. Yeats. After a good browse, she had once again been able to refresh her mind and soul with good art and then enjoy lunch and a read of the *Irish Times* in the gallery's 'With Taste' café. Thus culturally refreshed, she left the building by the Merrion Square West exit and crossed to Merrion Square Park to seek out the statue of Oscar Wilde. As she viewed this languorous figure sprawled on a Massive rock, she noticed, not far from her, two men in some kind of fractious discussion. The one who was facing in her direction had a shaved head, a face like a bulldog and a scar on his left cheek. Then she froze. The other one, she made out in profile, was her husband, Gerry.

She looked away as he glanced round in her direction. Had he recognised her? She did not wait to find out. She walked swiftly to the park exit and then ran as fast as she could down Merrion Square West, into and across Clare Street narrowly avoiding being knocked down by a passing van whose startled driver voiced a string of obscenities from his open window. A bus had just drawn up at a stop. It was a southbound 7A. She jumped aboard just as the door was closing. As the bus set off, heart thumping, Frances climbed the stair and hiding her face, behind her *Irish Times*, looked back out of a right hand window. At the corner of Merion Square stood Gerry Flynn scanning each of the four roads that converged at that point.

The bus trundled towards Dublin's south eastern suburbs through Booterstown, exactly in the opposite direction from Finbarr's house. At Blackrock, Frances got off the bus. Blackrock is a coastal commercial and commuter suburb and it has a station on the frequent Dublin Area Rapid Transit, or DART, electric line, that follows Dublin Bay from the south, through the City Centre to the north where the second last station is Portmarnock. The fugitive sister bought a ticket, caught the next northbound train and by this means she had doubled back to reach Finbarr's house in less than an hour.

* * *

Since that fateful moment in the park, Frances had been gripped by fear of her husband somehow intercepting her before she could escape. Of course he knew where Finbarr lived, so she could not stay there any longer. She had to put distance between herself and Dublin. But why was Gerry in Dublin? How could he have known she was there? Had he seen her in the park? Who was that unsavoury looking man he had been talking to? It was all so inexplicable, and worse – frightening.

By five o clock, Frances was on the road again. She had packed, loaded the car, and phoned Finbarr at his office to explain the close encounter with Gerry at

Merrion Square Park, her flight and her decision to head north-west to County Donegal. She had phoned her mother too at Letterkenny to announce her imminent arrival.

Once onto the M1 toll motorway heading north, her composure returned to a more settled condition. She would stay with her mother for a few days; perhaps visit some of her relations in Gweedore, and maybe Finbarr and Imelda could come up for the weekend. One way or the other, it would give her a chance to think things through and plan a future course of action.

She exited the motorway between Drogheda and Dundalk, drove through Ardee and up the N2 past Castleblaney and Monaghan to cross the border into Northern Ireland at Aughnacloy. Onwards she pressed up the A5 through Omagh and Strabane, crossing the River Foyle back into the Republic at Lifford Bridge to reach her mother's front door and a big motherly hug at half past eight.

The ensuing week in County Donegal was the tonic Frances needed to recover from the roller coaster of emotions she had recently experienced. Her mother was in good health and spirits which pleased Frances and the pair of them went over to Gweedore for three nights to visit their numerous relations on the O'Brien side of the family. The mixture of welcoming Gaelic speaking kin and the untamed magnificence of west Donegal blotted out the dark shadow of Gerry Flynn and restored the old Francie McGarrigle as the locals still called her.

On the Saturday, back in Letterkenny, Frances decided to go into Derry for the afternoon and evening for shopping and perhaps to take in a theatre or a traditional music pub or whatever turned up. The walled city of Derry, or Londonderry as it is known by many in the Loyalist community, is a lively centre for both County Donegal in the Republic and Counties of Derry and Tyrone in Northern Ireland.

A prowl round the shops yielded a chunky pair of buckled Spanish leather boots, a checked shirt, a green dress and silver chain belt. She put her haul in the boot of the car and then back in Bishop Street, at 'Don's' she bought fish and chips wrapped in a newspaper to take away to eat *al fresco* overlooking the city from its famous walls. Perched there, as she tucked in to this simple but tasty repast, she looked at the paper. It was a page from a week old copy of the *Sunday Sketch*. Her eye was drawn to the headline:

MONK MIRED IN MURDER MYSTERY.

A T DALMANNOCH, cleaning up proceeded room by room, interspersed by visits to the recycling centre. These visits began to take the form of social occasions as Brother Richard became known to the operatives there. They kept aside items that they thought might be of interest to their unusual client. In this way the busy monk picked up more chairs, two wardrobes, a double bed in almost new condition, sundry cabinets, a large and extremely heavy mahogany chest of drawers and even an electric organ.

Jamie Arbuckle had come and eventually gone off in his chic red two-seater, promising to return in future. The next day the man from Scotia Energy turned up, checked the meter, replaced it with a more modern circuit breaker box, muttered about the questionable state of the wiring, and promised power connection within twenty four hours. To his credit he reappeared within this timescale and to his and Brother Richard's relief, electrical power was restored to the old building without any bang, blue flash or other calamity. In fact the building had been largely rewired around 1975, and while the circuitry would, according to Jamie, need attention, it would serve adequately enough for the time being.

With power now available, Brother Richard turned his attention to the kitchen. It was a sizable room designed in earlier times to prepare meals for large numbers by labour intensive methods. It was dominated by a large deal table, but the room was equipped with a number of labour saving appliances, albeit now somewhat outmoded. Of these the electric hob and oven were tested and found to be functioning. At last the primus stove could be put away and more effective cooking methods employed.

Then there was the matter of hot water. Washing in cold water was certainly bracing, but a hot bath after several hard days' physical work seemed like a desirable recompense. The old building was fitted with an old fashioned solid fuel central heating system but did it still work? To start it up in the middle of summer was an extravagance too far, but an electric immersion over-ride for the hot water tank would generate hot water without engaging the whole system. A switch for such a device was found behind the kitchen press door. Brother Richard tried it. A red light came on, and in half an hour, after running the hot tap for a minute, piping hot water emitted.

That evening after a quick visit to town for supplies, sheets and a duvet for the newly acquired bed, the contented monk had a hot bath, cooked a chicken curry followed by fresh fruit salad, made his customary evening visit to the chapel and fell asleep in the made up double bed he had installed in the large front bedroom, or former dormitory to the right of the upstairs landing. No more indoor camping.

On the next morning, the postman arrived at Dalmannoch to make the first delivery of mail that Brother Richard had received since his arrival. It was a single letter from the lawyers, Agnew, Douglas and McWhirter, indicating that the funeral of their senior partner, Alexander Agnew would take place at 11AM on the following Wednesday at Mochrum, the village in which Mr Agnew had resided. Brother Richard made a mental note to attend.

By Saturday a good deal of progress had been made in cleaning and airing the building. The musty smells had largely disappeared and, while the wallpaper, paintwork and general décor looked tired and in need of a serious make-over, the building was beginning to take on a lived-in feel. Around mid-morning a small silver Peugeot hatch-back drew up by the front door. As Brother Richard went to investigate, two young men emerged. One was tall and thin with a somewhat lugubrious expression, the other smaller but stocky with trim beard, moustache and twinkling eyes.

"Hello. Brother Richard? asked the smaller of the two, who seemed to act as main spokesman."

The monk nodded and the new arrivals spoke alternately.

"We had a meeting last Friday with Professor Macdonald."

"Aye, a week ago, that is."

"He told us about what you were doing here."

"At Dalmannoch – your renovation work."

"We wondered if we could help."

"We dinna want peyd or onything, but . . ."

"But we have some ideas."

Brother Richard was slightly bemused: "Well you had better come in." And he took the newcomers through to the kitchen with the now inevitable offer of tea. "Now, let's hear what you have to say for yourselves."

"I'm Douglas Gordon," said the smaller and stockier of the two. "And I'm Gordon Douglas," said the other. Brother Richard raised an eyebrow and smiled;

"Now you're having me on."

"No, no joke," insisted Douglas, "I know it must seem funny, but Gordon and Douglas are common surnames <u>and</u> Christian names in Galloway".

Douglas continued: "We're both members of the Galloway Gaelic Group. In Gaelic that's 'Grunnan, Gàidhlig Ghallghaidhealaibh' or GGG for short. We are interested in the Celtic heritage of Galloway and have set up an 'Ùlpan' class."

This was all going a bit too fast for Brother Richard to take in. "Hold on: tea's ready. Explain all to a simple monk – Gaelic Group? – 'Ùlpan'? – your ideas?"

Between them the stocky Douglas and lugubrious Gordon explained that the Gaelic language, whilst quite widely spoken in parts of the Scottish Highlands and Islands, and indeed currently undergoing something of a renaissance, was once also prevalent in Galloway. It had, however, fallen out of general use in the area around the beginning of the 18th century. Elucidating further, they described how echoes of that Gaelic heritage remained, in hundreds, indeed thousands, of place-names, customs and beliefs and that they sought to re-learn the venerable language that had lain behind this rich heritage. The 'Ùlpan' method was a Gaelic language immersion scheme, recently introduced to Scotland, that promised steady progress to fluency and the GGG was fortunate in having a native Gaelic speaking tutor trained in this technique.

When they had met with Professor Macdonald, it had become apparent that he had been interested in the work of the group in researching the area's heritage and in their progress in learning the language. It was he who had suggested that there might be merit in helping Brother Richard achieve his purposes while possibly providing a meeting place for the group.

"Ye see," explained Gordon in his doleful way; "We hae oor regular meetings in a hotel in Castle Douglas but they hae jist pit their prices up. We wondered if we brocht the gang round tae help ye here at Dalmannoch, we could . . . weel maybe . . . hold a Gaelic immersion coorse or twa here."

"Of course," added Douglas, "We'll bring food and cook it for all of us."

It seemed to Brother Richard to be a reasonable offer worth putting to the test. It was therefore agreed that the following weekend, a gang of Gaelic learners would descend on Dalmannoch in an attempt to make a real impact on sprucing up the old building. For the rest of that Saturday, as an earnest of their intent, Douglas Gordon and Gordon Douglas set to in clearing out a couple of the upstairs rooms in the back wing that had not so far been tackled.

"I'm a plumber, by the way," declared Gordon as they prepared to leave; "I'd be happy to check oot the central heating system."

"Oh, one other thing," Douglas threw in; "Our tutor is a Church of Scotland minister. I hope that's all right with you; I mean with you being a Catholic and all that. He's very broad minded – for a minister."

"I'd be honoured to host a minister of the Scottish Church. In fact I'd be very interested to chat with him. You know, I'm quite broad minded myself – for a monk – maybe too broad minded."

With that the two young men departed.

* * *

Sunday was wet. It featured morning and evening visits to the chapel, Mass with Father Tom McGuire and a phone call to Prior John Ainslie with a progress report. Otherwise it was a day of quiet contemplation of matters both spiritual and secular. In the week since he had left

Father Tom, so much had happened. On the spiritual side, he had begun to feel real affection for the extraordinary little chapel at Dalmannoch that seemed to invoke weird and wonderful ideas. He would be interested in the Church of Scotland minister's impression of this strange building. On the secular side good progress had been made in cleaning up. Power was on. Jamie Arbuckle was in the clear, or so it seemed, and he awaited the outcome of a hoard of Gaelic students descending on him the following week-end. It was with these thoughts that he fell asleep on the recently installed double bed in the big front bedroom.

By Monday the weather had improved. Most of the main building had been cleaned and it was time to consider at least some up-grade of the décor. As he gave thought to options he continued with cleaning the furthest recesses of the east wing.

It was mid afternoon. The sun was out and Brother Richard was outside piling up accumulated debris from the last few days. Then along the drive, emerging from the wood, a car approached – a yellow Renault Megane. It drew up at the front door. The driver's door opened. Out stepped a dark haired woman. His heart missed a beat. It was Frances Flynn.

She stood for a moment and then ran towards the transfixed monk. The two hugged and kissed – and kissed and hugged.

O H, AM I GLAD I FOUND YOU! I thought I'd
never ever see you again." Frances nuzzled her
head against the monk's neck. "It's just so good
to see you."

"You know I was very worried about you,"
Brother Richard confessed; "Very worried. The night
before I left for Scotland – it seems like years ago now –
I heard that you had left Meadow View and no one knew
where you had gone. But let me look at you." He stood
back a little and looked at her. She seemed different –
dressed in a blue and cream checked shirt, neat blue
jeans with a silver chain belt and short chunky buckled
Spanish boots – but her demeanour was different – she
was smiling a broad smile, as though greatly thrilled and
relieved, yet there was the hint of a dark cloud there that
he had not observed before.

"It's so good to see you too. You look so – well
so beautiful. And look at me; I'm like a hobo in
these . .", and with his hand he tried to brush down his
dusty work-clothes."

At that the nurse said, "Oh no, you look just
stunning to me – just stunning – rugged and handsome.
But are you not going to invite me in Richard?"

"Of course, yes, of course. Come in and welcome
to Dalmannoch. It's a bit shabby, but at least it's a lot
cleaner than it was when I got here. Let me show you
round."

The tour moved from room to room and in
passing the kitchen, the customary kettle was filled and
placed on the hob. Frances gave Richard a sly look as
she observed the double bed in the best bedroom, in

response to which he gave a nervous cough and extolled the fruits of the recycling centre.

Back in the kitchen tea was infused, to which Frances suggested; "Why don't we have something a little stronger." She went out to the car and returned with a bottle of Paddy Irish Whiskey to announce; "I think this reunion calls for a celebration." She poured two generous measures. "Sláinte ! Now tell me what have you been up to? What's all this about a murder? I read about it in the *Sunday Sketch* and you being beaten up by the police or something."

"I'm surprised you read the *Sunday Sketch*."

"I don't, but my fish and chips were wrapped up in it. I couldn't help it."

"Well yes there was a murder here. I discovered the body. The police questioned me for a long time but in the end were happy enough to let me go. There was no brutality. In fact the Inspector – a man called Morrison – was quite civil and reasonable. The *Sketch* reporter, what's his name – Shaw – has, it seems, a talent for exaggeration."

Brother Richard then described, in brief, the sequence of events since his fight with Gerry Flynn right up until Frances' arrival at Dalmannoch.

"But," addressing Frances; "More to the point where have you been. What have you been up to?"

Frances Flynn described how her own life had been so drastically affected since that fateful day at Meadow View. Brother Richard was gratified to hear about the apparent progress with Tom Bayliss's grandson Darren. He was amazed and concerned to hear the account of Frances flight to Ireland to escape from her husband's demand for money. Frances explained the gist of her predicament.

"You see I have inherited a fair slug of cash. Sure it's in the bank in my own name. But I'm still married to Gerry. My big fear is that, as my husband he'll somehow manage to get his filthy hands on it. He's violent; he's a gambler and getting desperate. He's mortgaged to the hilt on his semi and owes, goodness knows how much in gambling debts to the Casino de Oro in Bristol. It's owned by a businessman called Billy Wilson who has put the squeeze on Gerry. From what I hear, this Billy Wilson is ruthless. He's basically a gangster originally from Glasgow and they say involved in the drug trade. That's why I don't want Gerry to find me until I can find some way to protect myself and my assets. I'm very frightened Richard."

Brother Richard put a reassuring arm round Frances' shoulder.

"You're safe here. We'll find a way through this." He poured Frances another dram from her bottle. "It's a bit basic here but you're welcome to stay. I don't know what Prior John would say but, hey, he's four hundred miles away."

In fact the monk had a pretty good idea of the prior's likely attitude but was buoyed by the sense that he, Brother Richard, made the decisions here. He considered that, just as Father McGuire had taken him into his house in time of need, it would, he argued, be justifiable to do the same for Sister Frances.

Frances took a sip of Paddy. "My brother Finbarr's an accountant in Dublin; and he's smart. He reckons that it may be possible to put my funds beyond Gerry's reach by finding a suitable investment vehicle. But before we could explore that further, I spotted Gerry in Dublin arguing over some deal with a horrible looking man. B' Jayssus, I ran for it and managed to get away on a bus. I don't know if Gerry spotted me or not, but I think he might have. Anyway I went up to Letterkenny to stay with my Mam. Then when I was on a trip to Derry on Saturday, I bought fish and chips wrapped in an old copy of the *Sunday Sketch*, and there was this article about you. Well, apart from the police brutality, it mentioned that you were renovating a monastery called Dalmannoch, near Whithorn, in South West Scotland. So I decided to come here and booked the ferry yesterday and caught the fast P&O boat from Larne to Cairnryan and here I am. I hope you don't mind."

"Mind? I'm delighted. It's just wonderful to see you. As you'll see Dalmannoch is no monastery, just a former retreat house. Now let's put your troubles behind you and pull together some grub. Why don't we go into Wigtown and get some better fare than the basics I have here and we can prepare a meal fit for a queen. You can unpack when we get back."

Monk and sister set off in Frances' Megane, bought a leg of Scotch lamb, a favourite of Frances, wine, other ingredients, cut flowers and tall red candles. Back at Dalmannoch, the old kitchen delivered the promised royal meal, over which Richard described the joys of his childhood, the sorrow of his youth and his varied career before entering Whitleigh. Frances regaled her own happy childhood and her, at times riotous interlude at Liverpool. More recent events were left unmentioned.

When the sweet course of chocolate mousse with cream was devoured, they repaired to the common room where Richard lit a fire. Frances switched on the electric organ that had been retrieved from the recycling centre. It functioned and Frances played and sang some old favourite Irish songs in both English and Irish Gaelic to the admiration of Richard. He in turn sang sea shanties

94

and Cornish songs learned in his young days in the West Country. It was a gloriously happy evening with many a laugh that continued much later than Brother Richard was recently accustomed.

When bed time came, it was arranged that Frances would have the double bed in the main room and Richard would revert to the camp bed in the smaller room next door. And each repaired to their respective quarters.

As Richard lay in the dark on his camp bed, recalling with contentment the unexpected events of the day, he heard a voice from the room next door.

"Richard. Are you awake? – Good – me too. I've been on my own for too long. Come in beside me."

A MORNING EXCURSION

THAT MORNING; the morning after Frances' arrival at Dalmannoch, Brother Richard rose later than usual, but earlier than the woman with whom he had shared the night. The sun shone. There was much to consider, yet he felt good; better than he had felt for a long time. That morning too, the interior of the little chapel seemed to dance in radiant multi-coloured light. Perhaps it was the angle at which the sun penetrated the stained glass at this later hour. Whatever the cause, it had a distracting, even bewitching, effect on one monk who perchance sought guilt but could not find it.

Back in the kitchen he was joined by Frances. "Good morning my lovely Richard." She offered him a little kiss – a kiss he accepted and returned

"It IS a good morning", the monk responded, "and how is the lovely Frances Flynn today?" On eliciting a positive answer to this enquiry, breakfast of porridge, orange juice, tea and toast was prepared and eaten.

"You know Richard; I have been in Ireland where people have always known me as Frances McGarrigle. I'd like to revert to my maiden name. After all nobody here knows me.

"That's fine by me Frances McGarrigle," agreed Brother Richard, adding, "and I was thinking; I have to get rid of some stuff at the recycling centre. You could come with me, and . . ."

"Oo, the dump ! Lovely ! You say the most romantic things," quipped Frances with a twinkle in her eye."

"No, no," protested Richard; "Well in fact the recycling centre is an interesting place, but no, what I mean is; after the 'dump', we could go and have a look at Whithorn and Isle of Whithorn and maybe have lunch there. They're not far. I think you'd enjoy the outing. I haven't been back myself since I met up with Professor Macdonald the day after I arrived here."

After breakfast they loaded the van with the debris from the previous few days work and headed for the recycling centre to deposit the said material. The operatives were as friendly as ever. The foreman was a large ruddy faced mature man called Wullie.

"There's nae muckle o' interest the day Brither Richard, bit we'll keep oor een oot and let ye ken gin there's onie guid pieces." Brother Richard thanked the foreman and introduced Frances. "Aye, weel ye're baith welcome onie time. Gin ye tak things awa, it aye helps us turn things roon. We hae tae dae aa we can tae reduce the landfill tax the cooncil his tae pey."

After several visits, Brother Richard had begun to get the hang of Wullie's, at first, impenetrable vernacular, and was indeed still not quite managing total comprehension. He was a little surprised to find that Frances had understood Wullie's monologue quite well, on account, apparently, of long-established links between County Donegal and Scotland.

The next call was Whithorn where they stopped at the visitor centre, museum and the ruins of the old priory. Richard proudly showed Frances the collection of carved stones and other artefacts, previously described by Professor Macdonald, and did his best to recall and impart their significance.

As they took in the presentations, Frances was as fascinated as Richard had been; to learn that here the first recorded Christian church in Scotland was built by St Ninian, a Briton, around 400 AD. It had been called, in Latin *Candida Casa*, meaning white house. The Anglians had translated this as as *Hwit Ærne*, which evolved into the modern name Whithorn. A monastery and diocese of the Anglian kingdom of Northumbria was created on the site in the eighth century and later revived by the Gaelic Fergus, Lord or King of Galloway and equally Gaelic Bishop Gille-Aldan from the twelfth century. Frances marvelled at the exquisit gilded and enamelled Whithorn crozier on loan from the National Museums of Scotland with its outstanding champlevé enamels. This relic was thought to have been buried with the body of Simon de Wedale, one of Whithorn's bishops in the twelfth century. For such a small, out-of-the-way place, Frances couldn't help but sense that little Whithorn carried a colorful and disproportionate weight of pomp and history as she tried to visualise what life had been like when the town was in its heyday.

Before leaving the historic Royal Burgh, a guide to Whithorn and its Priory and a copy of the weekly *Galloway Gleaner* were purchased at the nearby newsagent and ten minutes later the van was parked at the same Isle of Whithorn harbour road-end location as on Brother Richard's first uncomfortable night in Scotland.

The harbour looked much the same as it did on that following morning, except that the neat wooden cutter was no longer there.

"Let me show you the view from the top of the hill." The pair strode up to the view point where Brother Richard had met Professor Macdonald. Once they had reached it, they beheld that same 360° panorama.

"That's the Isle of Man out there." The monk indicated with his finger.

"I was there once with my parents when I was a girl. We had a lovely time," recalled Frances. "Happy memories; I always meant to go back again."

"I wonder if that can be arranged from here," pondered Richard.

Having taken in all that was to be seen of the view, the Steam Packet Inn and lunch was the next objective of the jaunt. The dining room was fairly quiet and the couple settled down; Richard scanning the Whithorn guide-book, Frances scrutinizing the *Galloway Gleaner*.

"This is very interesting," declared the monk engrossed in his book, "Professor Macdonald told me that the shrine of St Ninian was an internationally renowned place of pilgrimage. He wasn't joking. It says here the priory was visited by Edward II of England, and Scottish Kings Robert The Bruce , David II, James I, III, IV (many times), James V and Mary Queen of Scots" before it was disbanded after the Reformation."

After a period of silent reading Frances countered: "Listen to this in the *Gleaner*; the front page story says: 'On Saturday evening, police seized a large consignment of crack cocaine at the ferry port of Cairnryan, thought to have a street value of £60,000. A man has been detained in connection with the incident. It is understood that this was only one of a recent series of shipments destined from Ireland to Glasgow'. You know I have been wondering if that man Gerry was arguing with in Dublin was some kind of drug dealer. My brother Finbarr told me that a huge shipment of Columbian crack cocaine had been landed in Ireland and the Irish market was too small to handle it, especially since the financial crisis.

Apparently the Irish criminal fraternity has been exporting it to the UK."

"Mm, I hope you're wrong about Gerry", thought Brother Richard. "From what I know about that business, it's very nasty.

There are soft drugs and hard drugs. Some are not particularly addictive, but crack cocaine and heroin are seriously bad news."

Each returned to their reading and then Frances broke in; "It seems the drug trade is not the only crooked activity in these parts. Here's a story about a property developer Edward North who has been accused of trying to bribe councillors to approve a housing development. One of the councillors, an Andrew Dunbar, reported the man to the police and now this North man is denying the accusation."

"North?" enquired the monk, "That's the man Jamie Arbuckle said the police had been asking him about when they questioned him."

Then, after a further silence, Frances again announced. "Look, here's the notice for Alexander Agnew's funeral."

"Poor man," pondered Brother Richard as he looked at the notice, "I wish I had actually met him in life. He seems to have been a very honourable man. At least we can show our respects tomorrow."

Lunch was then served and enjoyed over lighter and more enjoyable topics of conversation.

As they prepared to return to Dalmannoch, Brother Richard took Frances' arm and looked over the calm and picturesque little harbour of Isle of Whithorn and to the green countryside beyond and declared:

"Despite all the recent shocks, puzzles and problems, I'm beginning to like this place – especially since you have arrived Frances McGarrigle."

The Steam Packet Inn at Isle of Whithorn

HECTOR WOODROW-DOUGLAS

T HEY HAD NOT BEEN LONG back at
Dalmannoch, when a grey Land Rover Recovery
drew up and out stepped a tall late middle aged
distinguished looking man in a well pressed light suit,
tan brogues, dark blue shirt and blending tartan tie. He
held out his hand to shake Richard's:

"Hi there! Are you Brother Richard?" His accent
had a transatlantic flavour, although not strongly so. "I'm
Hector Woodrow-Douglas. I'm a trustee of the
Dalmannoch trust. Catriona Macarthur at Agnew,
Douglas and McWhirter told me you would be here. It's
good to see the old place being spruced up."

"I'm very pleased to meet you, Mr Woodrow-
Douglas . . ."

"Please, no ceremony. Just call me Hector," said
the new arrival.

"Well Hector, as I said, I'm pleased to see you.
I'd welcome a bit of background on the Dalmannoch
Trust and indeed some advice as to . . . But how bad
mannered of me, talking to you on the doorstep. Please
come inside." The two men went to the common room
where Frances was polishing the electric organ. Brother
Richard introduced her with:

"This is my friend Frances McGarrigle. She's has
just come over from Ireland to – em – lend a hand.
Frances this is Hector Woodrow-Douglas. He's a trustee
of the Dalmannoch trust."

"Nice to meet you, Mr Douglas . . ."

"Nice to meet you too, Frances, but 'Hector', will
be fine."

"All right, can I get you both a cup of tea?

"Do you have coffee?" enquired Hector.

"Yes of course, coffee it is. Milk? Sugar?

"Just black, thanks."

As Frances disappeared to the kitchen, Brother Richard gestured to Hector Woodrow-Douglas to take a seat and awaited an explanation as to the purpose of his visit. This was forthcoming as follows.

"As I said Brother Richard, I'm one of the three trustees of the Dalmannoch Trust. You probably know of the others. They are Bishop Wilfred Newman and the legal firm of Agnew, Douglas and McWhirter. I was stunned to hear about the death of Alexander Agnew, or Alec as he was known to his friends – and I regarded him as a good friend. I have known him for many years – decades in fact – and had a great deal of respect for him. It's difficult to believe that his death was the result of foul play – terrible – just terrible. I sure couldn't miss his funeral tomorrow. That, however, is not my only reason for my being back in Scotland.

Brother Richard, the fact that you are here working on Dalmannoch indicates that you are aware that the trustees have been looking at the possible disposal of the buildings and, indeed, Alec indicated your role to me before he died. I have, of course, been in correspondence with the trustees over the last six months and more, about this proposed course of action and have to say that I have all along had some concerns about the whole business. Since Alec's death, I am now most anxious that the original purpose of the trust is protected."

At this point, Frances appeared with the beverages accompanied by a plate loaded with slices of cherry and sultana cake. She laid them out on the coffee table and made ready to remove herself from what was evidently a confidential discussion. Brother Richard stopped her.

"Hector, I think it would be useful for Frances to join us. She is aware of my work here and as a nursing sister you can be confident of her discretion. I think I should explain that my instructions from my prior at Whitleigh Priory are twofold: firstly to tidy the building up, and secondly to find a prospective buyer who will carry forward the spiritual purpose of the trust. I am making some progress with the first, but how the second can be achieved is – well I have no idea what to do. I would welcome any thoughts you may have. In fact you are the first trustee I have actually met – alive – that is to say."

"Fine, that's OK," continued the visitor, "Let me now explain the background. My family is descended from the Black Douglas who was King Robert the Bruce's right-hand-man in achieving success in Scotland's struggle to regain independence in the early fourteenth century. Our branch is a minor strand of that line. However, one of my ancestors, who helped King James IV escape an attempted assassination, while on pilgrimage to Whithorn, by hiding him under his green cloak, was granted land in the Machars. We have been known since then as the Green Douglases and like many lesser landed families we have had our ups and downs.

My great grandfather, Sir Joseph Douglas, was an antiquarian with an interest in ancient cults, rites, and myths and in particular in all things Celtic. Notwithstanding his academic interests he was something of a dashing fellow and he married a wealthy English heiress, Lady Mary Blundell from the Cotswold area who subsequently inherited a sizable estate around the village of Wethercott St Giles. Anyway she was a

Catholic and in recognition of her spiritual persuasion, Joseph built and endowed Dalmannoch, under the terms of a trust – the Dalmannoch Trust – as a place of Catholic retreat, but also as a place that recognised and celebrated the other aspects of Galloway's rich and ancient spiritual and cultural heritage. With all that in mind he designed the Dalmannoch Trust so as to ensure the continuance of both of these purposes.

The wealth accumulated by my great grandfather was dissipated in time by extravagant living and by death duties. I had to make my own way in the world and, as a young man, and younger son, I emigrated to Canada. I built up a freight forwarding business in Vancouver and it has done quite well – I guess it's due to a combination of luck and hard work. My older brother James, had numerous female attachments, but never married. He was killed in a motor racing accident and so, by default as it were, I became chief of our small clan; for what it is now worth.

You see my brother liked the high-life and took little interest in Dalmannoch or in family or heritage. Since his death, however, I have developed an interest in these things and in particular in the work of my great grandfather, Sir Joseph. I discovered that he knew people like William Morris, John Ruskin, James George Frazer and William G Collingwood; great thinkers, writers and antiquarians of the late Victorian and Edwardian period and I have become a bit of an antiquarian myself.

That's why I want to try to keep the spirit of Dalmannoch alive."

"Well, I'd like to think we could help you achieve that aim," Brother Richard volunteered, "although I don't know quite how. I have been concentrating on cleaning the place since I arrived. You know it was in a bit of a mess when I started."

"Oh, I know, Brother Richard. I have visited Dalmannoch many times – and recently on every occasion I have come over to Scotland. Of course I knew the place as a young man when it was still operational. It has been disheartening to see it going to rack and ruin. So, Brother Richard, all credit to you and your efforts."

The monk asked the Canadian if he had any ideas as to how the 'spirit' of Dalmannoch could actually be saved.

"Well yes and no. I have some ideas, but, as yet, no firm plan. You see, the Bishop is pushing for a sale to raise money for his diocese. I am not keen unless, as I have said, the spiritual purpose of the place can be assured. Alec was sympathetic to my own view, but tipped me the wink that a real estate developer – a Mr. Edward North was interested in the site. The trouble is; by all accounts this North guy is a crook and any promises or undertakings he might make on protecting the function of Dalmannoch, would almost certainly be broken. So, apart from Alec's funeral, I want to see if an alternative purchaser can be found – or, if needs be – created.

THE FUNERAL OF ALEXANDER AGNEW

T HE DAY of Alexander Agnew's funeral was overcast and threatening to rain. Brother Richard and Sister Frances set off in Frances' car for the small village of Mochrum where the service was to be held. As a token of respect Brother Richard, donned his monk's habit and scapular while Frances wore her blue Sister's uniform. By the time they arrived at about half past ten, it was already quite difficult to find a parking place, such were the numbers who had already turned up for the service.

Mochrum is on the west side of the Machars peninsula. The Main Street features a long row of terraced cottages, but the centrepiece of the village is the kirk; a prime example of a Scottish post-Reformation church, but built on the site of a twelfth century building.

Having found a place to leave the car, Richard and Frances joined a growing procession making its way towards the kirk. As they entered, an elder handed them a leaflet with the order of service. They chose a pew near the back of the church. By this time it was quarter to eleven and the building was already quite full. The contrast with the highly decorated chapel at Dalmannoch could hardly have been greater. In true Presbyterian fashion the plain interior superseded any concession to aesthetics. Brother Richard noted, with interest, the simple, clear glazed arched windows, the undecorated ceiling and the balconies that cut across the windows regardless of architectural sensitivity. The 'Word' being all important; the pulpit dominated, set high on the south wall between two windows.

By eleven, the church was full. Among those foregathered, he recognised, Hector Woodrow-Douglas. Sitting with others, doubtless colleagues from Agnew, Douglas and McWhirter, were Catriona Macarthur and Betty MacDowell, then further back, sitting and talking with another group, Douglas Gordon and Gordon Douglas. On the pews, set at right angles, to the right of the pulpit, sat Robert Heron whom he had met at Tebay, and on the row behind, Inspector Morrison. Opposite them sat Wullie, foreman at the recycling centre. Clearly Alexander Agnew was a well respected figure in the local community.

At the appointed time the beadle brought the bible to the pulpit. The minister then appeared and mounted the steps to take charge of events. Brother Richard, brought up as a Methodist, had a good grasp of the Protestant approach, but held the opinion that the Scottish version would be altogether more severe. As the service progressed, he was pleasantly surprised at the simple humanity of the sermon, the appropriateness of the hymns and the dignity of the accolades given by James McCulloch, now senior partner of the firm and of one of the local councillors, Andrew Dunbar.

The tragic circumstances of Alexander Agnew's death were recognised, but at least he was getting a worthy send-off to the next world. As the service unfolded, Brother Richard recalled finding the lawyer's body and the subsequent hostile questioning by the police. He recalled too Jamie Arbuckle's frightening experience and wondered who could have a motive to impersonate the architect and lure the much loved lawyer to his death. Mostly he regretted that he had not met Alexander Agnew while he had been alive. He was certain he would have both enjoyed his company and

108

benefited from his advice as to how to proceed with the disposal of Dalmannoch.

At the end of the service, the pallbearers carried the coffin through the church to the adjacent church yard and its ancient cemetery where the open grave had been prepared. A piper played 'Flowers of the Forest'. A soft drizzle was falling. Brother Richard and Frances observed from a discrete distance:

"Ashes to ashes – dust to dust . . ."
Hector Woodrow-Douglas and a few other men were then seen one by one to cast what looked like leafy twigs into the open grave as a piper played a strangely haunting but beautiful lament. Most of those present were visibly moved, many, men included, were unashamedly in tears.

At a signal from the minister, the assembly started to disperse towards their vehicles to head for The Monreith Arms Hotel, a former coaching inn, in nearby Port William where a buffet reception was provided.

As invitees entered the establishment, they offered their condolences to Alexander Agnew's sister Alice Powell and her husband Bruce who had travelled from Australia and, as the company settled, the mood changed to that of animated conviviality. Old friends met old friends, anecdotes were exchanged and the general feeling of relief, after the emotional tension of the service, coupled with a lacing of whisky, fuelled an atmosphere of joviality; hilarity even, with which Brother Richard felt slightly uneasy.

As he looked round the kaleidoscope of gossiping groups, he observed, what was clearly the legal fraternity; then there was the farming community, broadly spoken, with which Alexander Agnew had done much business;

and there were assorted others, presumably friends or relations who wished to show their respects.

Notwithstanding their prevalence in the past, monks are not a commonplace sight these days in the Machars of Galloway. The presence, therefore, at the reception, of a young well built monk in full monkish attire, with an attractive dark haired uniformed nursing sister as consort, made something of a surreal, perhaps even suggestive, impression upon some of the assembled company. In fact, whispering from the corner of his mouth, a wise-cracker in a far corner of the room wondered if the pair was bound for a 'vicars and tarts' party. Poorly suppressed chortles erupted among those in the immediate vicinity; fortunately unnoticed by Brother Richard and Sister Frances.

In a more central part of the room, Catriona Macarthur, took it upon herself to introduce Brother Richard to a number of those assembled, and was in turn introduced to Sister Frances. Among those thus brought together, was Robert Heron.

"Brother Richard and I have already met. It's such a pity our second meeting is in these unfortunate circumstances. How are things progressing at Dalmannoch?"

"Oh, there has been quite a lot to do in just cleaning the place up, but good progress has been made. The next stage – the future of the building – is more of a puzzle. There seem to be differing ideas about the way forward." Brother Richard felt it unwise to go into any further detail.

Smiling at Catriona Macarthur, Robert Heron advised, "Well you will be in good hands with Catriona – Miss Macarthur – looking after your interests. I'll be very interested to hear how things turn out."

Catriona Macarthur smiled back. "I'll do my best Robbie, but I have had a fair bit of detective work to do in sorting out Alec's notes – as you know, he wasn't the tidiest of souls."

"Miss Macarthur has been very helpful and efficient," Brother Richard confirmed to the pleasure of both Catriona and 'Robbie', "But talking of detective work, I see Inspector Morrison there; I think I'll have a quick word with him." Leaving Frances with the two lawyers to be introduced round others of the company, he excused himself and made his way over to where the policeman was standing munching a ham roll.

"Hello, Inspector; how is the case progressing?"

"I'm afraid we have made no arrest as yet Brother Richard. We are still proceeding with our enquiries." The inspector was in no mood to divulge that, avenues of investigation had dried up, following the removal of Jamie Arbuckle from their suspicions.

Brother Richard volunteered: "I have been thinking, Inspector, about the person who presented himself as Jamie Arbuckle on the day Mr. Agnew was killed. It seems to me that awareness of a possible link between Jamie and Dalmannoch can only have originated from Whitleigh Priory or someone closely connected with it. I wonder if it would be worth your while making contact with the prior – Prior John Ainslie."

The inspector raised an eyebrow.

"Mm, I will bear your suggestion in mind Brother Richard. I may call round at Dalmannoch to ask you for a little more information about the priory. Meanwhile, I'm afraid I have my duties to attend to but thank you for taking the time to speak to me." And with that the inspector departed.

Brother Richard returned to Frances who was now speaking with a heavily built farmer and his wife.

"Aye weel, Alec Agnew or AA as some caad him, wiz a richt gentleman. He wiz verra helpfu' tae us ower oor boondary dispute wi thon evil bugger Jamie Dunbar. Is that no richt Bella?"

"He wiz that, Sandy", confirmed the burly, ample bosomed Bella.

"Och, here's me haiverin' awa aboot oor troubles," declared the farmer turning to Brother Richard, "And fae whit I hear, ye've hid a few o yer ain Brither Richard. Yer ledy-frien Frances here wiz telling me aa aboot ye. I'm Sandy McKie and this is ma guid-wife Bella. We hae a bittie fairm nae faur fae Sorbie. Ye'd aye be welcome gin ye wiz passin."

And so the somewhat one-sided conversation continued until monk and sister took their leave. The unlikely looking pair crossed the road from the hotel and made for the sea wall. There they stood side by side. Their hands touched, clasped and squeezed as confirmation of a growing mutual bond. In silence they stood, breathing the welcome sea air and taking in the view of Luce Bay and the long blue outline of the Mull of Galloway defining the clearing western horizon.

Their heads cleared and their spirits soothed, they headed back to Dalmannoch.

IT WAS ON THE LATE MORNING of the following day that Inspector Morrison called at Dalmannoch. He was accompanied by the same sergeant who had barred their entry while the forensic examination had been under way.

"Good morning Brother Richard," said the inspector, "You have already met Sergeant Watt." The sergeant nodded in response, as did Brother Richard.

"Yes indeed and good morning to you both. Come in, come in; you will see that the place has been tidied up a bit since you were last here." Brother Richard ushered the policemen into the common room and introduced Frances.

"This is Frances McGarrigle. She's helping me here. You possibly saw her yesterday at Mr. Agnew's funeral."

"Yes indeed. I'd say the pair of you made quite an impression yesterday", declared the inspector.

"That was certainly not our intention", averred Brother Richard slightly offended, and now back in his working clothes.

"Quite so," said the inspector with an understanding smile. Skilled detective that he was; it did not require the sleuthing skills of a Sherlock Holmes to deduce that there was more than just passing acquaintance in the relationship between monk and nurse.

"When we talked yesterday, you mentioned that the murder of Mr. Agnew may have some link with your priory – what's its name – White . . ."

"Whitleigh", confirmed Brother Richard. "I'm not saying one of the brothers was directly responsible –

no, not at all – but somehow, I can't help thinking that whoever claimed to be Jamie Arbuckle and, presumably enticed Mr Agnew away from his office to his death, had some connection with Whitleigh. You see Jamie oversaw a building project I was working on before I came here. I got to know him quite well and, as far as I know, he had never heard of Dalmannoch until a couple of weeks, or so, before I was sent here, and even then I can't see that he would have heard of Alexander Agnew at any time before you picked him up. Nor, I think, would anyone else, bar the prior. Admittedly, I suppose in those couple of weeks, quite a few knew where I was heading, and knew that Jamie was a Scottish based architect, linked with the priory."

At this juncture Sergeant Watt broke in; "But could Mr. Agnew no have kent Jamie Arbuckle was to be involved and maybe passed this knowledge on to somebody local?"

"It's possible George, I suppose", admitted the inspector. "We can have another go at Agnew, Douglas and McWhirter to see if we can uncover anything more, but there may be something in what Brother Richard says about Whitleigh."

In listening to this exchange, Brother Richard made a further contribution to what was developing as a debate. "I know nothing about police procedures, so forgive me if this seems naïve, but I understand that Mr Agnew was very discrete and rather unlikely to pass on information about a delicate and impending transaction to a non-involved third party. Even if he did, the original source would have to have been someone involved with Whitleigh. It does strike me, however, that as Miss Macarthur has taken over as the firm's representative on the Dalmannoch Trust, she is going through Mr Agnew's notes and she may be able to uncover some contact or phone number that would throw some light on the problem."

"Brother Richard, you are by no means naïve. Your suggestions are certainly worth considering and I thank you for them." The inspector continued: "Sergeant Watt and I will make contact with Whitleigh and with Miss Macarthur to see what we can uncover. If you have any further thoughts on the case please contact me."

The two policemen, who had been seated, stood with the intention of departing, when Frances McGarrigle broke in:

"There is one other thing I'd like to mention."

The inspector and sergeant sat down again.

"I'm not quite sure where to start but the main reason I'm here at Dalmannoch is that I am trying to keep clear of my husband. His name is Gerald Flynn. You see he's violent and demanding a large sum of money from me. Brother Richard was very helpful a couple of months ago in rescuing me when my husband assaulted me."

Frances then summarised the sequence of events in her attempts to avoid Gerry including the incident at Merrion Square Gardens in Dublin. Brother Richard added that he was keen to protect Frances in any way he could.

"I'm not asking for police protection, not at the moment at any rate, but I thought it would be useful for you to be informed of these circumstances – just in case.

"Let me get this straight Mrs. McGarrigle," the inspector seemed especially interested in Frances' story, while the sergeant made notes in his black note book, "you say your husband Gerald Flynn is being pressed to make good gambling debts incurred at a casino in Bristol. What was the name of the casino?"

"The Casino de Oro. It's owned by a Billy Wilson", confirmed Frances. "Gerry used to go there a lot – probably still does."

"And you say that you suspect your husband may be caught up in the drugs trade."

"Well I don't know that," explained Frances, "and again as far as I know he never took drugs himself; I'll give him credit for that. It's just a feeling I got when I saw him arguing with that man in Dublin. I might be wrong."

"Imph'm – aye – well, from the circumstances you describe, your husband may well have been pressed into the drugs business to pay off his debts. If Billy Wilson is who I think he is, he's a very nasty piece of work. If he's the Billy Wilson who left Glasgow seven or eight years ago, he's a brother of Jimmy Wilson a well known Glasgow gangster. He's been done for drugs before but his lawyer got him off on a technicality. When these fellows have a hold over you, they'll get you to do their dirty work like acting as long distance couriers – 'mules' they call them. And if the mule fouls up, these hoods are unforgiving – ruthless psychopaths most of them, and the Wilson brothers are no exception."

"No wonder he sees me as an easy way out of his problems", declared Frances. "After what you have said, I'm more frightened than ever now about what might happen if he catches up with me."

"I wouldn't worry too much Mrs McGarrigle. Your husband isn't likely to find you here. But what you told us may be helpful. If you or Brother Richard come across any other leads, either on the murder of Mr. Agnew or your husband's whereabouts, let me know.

Here's my phone number;" at which the inspector handed his card to Brother Richard.

After the police had left Frances and Richard looked at each other.

"Well we can't say they didn't listen to us," declared Brother Richard, I'm quite impressed by their thoroughness."

Frances agreed, although now more apprehensive than ever about Gerry's intentions towards her. Then it dawned on her that she hadn't offered the police tea.

"Oh I dare say they get plenty of tea in the course of their enquiries", suggested Brother Richard. "But, I've just thought, I never mentioned the bus ticket."

"Bus ticket?" enquired Frances

"Yes, when the professor and I went into the chapel for the first time I found a bus ticket under a pew. It was dated the first of May. I'd better mention it to the inspector next time I see him."

A S IT HAPPENED, the mystery of the bus ticket was explained the following day. Events started normally enough; Brother Richard with his morning devotional visit to the chapel, Frances preparing breakfast and the subsequent taking of the meal together.

It was mid morning as Brother Richard was outside at the front of Dalmannoch, scraping dried putty from the common room windows, when a puttering and aged Volkswagen Kombi minibus drew up. The vehicle bore all the stereotypical hallmarks of the legendary 'hippie van' of the 1960s; multi-coloured body work, wheel hubs painted as black and white yin-yang symbols and what looked like red woollen threads drooping from the aerial. Brother Richard was curious to see who might emerge from this improbable vehicle. In the event, the driver's door opened and a relatively normal looking well built man, in navy slacks and an open-necked cream linen shirt stepped out, walked towards the monk and held out his hand, enquiring:

"Hello. Are you Brother Richard Wells?"

"I am – and you are . . ?" responded the nonplussed Brother Richard.

"My name is Thomas Nutter – and yes I know it causes amusement, but that has been our family surname for centuries." Brother Richard resisted comment, other than;

"How can I help you Mr Nutter?"

"Well, Brother Richard, I am a member of the Wigtown Wicca Coven. I just wanted to let you know of our existence and to seek your co-operation in our continued use of Dalmannoch for our seasonal Sabbats."

Thomas Nutter spoke with an accent of the north of England and as the caller thus introduced himself, Brother Richard noticed that there were others in the minibus peering through the vehicle's numerous windows.

"I think you will need to tell me more about your group and its activities." Brother Richard stalled for time, "And perhaps you would ask the others of your passengers if they wish to join us."

"Yes certainly;" at which Thomas Nutter walked back to the extraordinary vehicle, opened the back door, commenced a brief conversation with the occupants, who then materialized one by one.

"Let me introduce these representatives of our coven. This is Holly Garden our Priestess." A tubby smiling grey-haired middle-aged woman took Brother Richard's hand with both of hers and held it for some seconds and announced:

"I'm very pleased to meet you Brother Richard. I would very much like to explain what we stand for and seek your understanding. We are ordinary folk who are following our particular spiritual path. We wish no-one harm."

Brother Richard noticed that she was wearing, as a pendant, a silver seven pointed Elven star identical to that pointed out by Professor Macdonald in the Dalmannoch chapel.

The others were then introduced by Holly Garden as: Emily Johnstone, a young auburn-haired woman; Jonathan Hepburn a young man with a pony tail and wearing a black tee-shirt bearing the same seven pointed star as that displayed by the priestess, and finally Suzie Silver, a stunning looking blonde-haired woman in her late twenties, wearing a short loose fitting white dress

119

held at the waist by a broad black leather belt set with silver Celtic knot-work medallions.

"I think you had better all come in and then you can explain the purpose of your visit." Brother Richard ushered the group into the common room as Frances appeared from the kitchen, saying:

"I thought I heard voices."

The company was introduced once more. Brother Richard admired Frances' straight-faced ability to show no sign of surprise or amusement at the somewhat bizarre assembly. He presumed this came from years of nursing in which she would have come across every conceivable and inconceivable type of character. Frances sat down awaiting developments and Brother Richard opened negotiations.

"Now Mrs Garden, tell me what this is all about."

"Holly; call me Holly. We use first names in the Craft. We are members of the Wigtown Wicca Coven. In other words we follow a dualistic Pagan religion in which we believe in the great complement, or some may say conflict, between the benevolent and the malignant. Most religious systems have some form of moral dualism; in Christianity, for instance, the conflict between good and evil. I should stress that we greatly respect those of the Christian persuasion, although Christianity has in the past been very intolerant of us and we have been cruelly persecuted, particularly here in Scotland.

Just as Christians have their moral code; so do we. Ours is expressed simply in the Wiccan Rede: 'If it harm none, do what ye will'. We also believe in the Law of the Threefold Return which means that whatever you do to another person or thing, benevolent or otherwise, it returns on you with triple force.

As with other religions we have our magic and our rituals. Our magic draws on the natural laws and we only practice it with those who wish to receive it. Our rituals are taken from the living Celtic Pagan traditions. You see, although the ancient Celtic religions and sites were largely subsumed by Christianity, many of the old traditions survived in the form of folklore, mythology, songs, and prayers in the Celtic lands of Ireland, Wales, Scotland, Cornwall and the Isle of Man. Our chief festivals are those of the wheel of the Celtic year. In the course of the year we have eight Sabbats, as we call them, of which four are fire festivals. Midsummer is one of our Sabbats and it is about that in particular that we wish to speak with you."

Brother Richard was quite taken aback by this exposition. The members of the Wigtown Wicca Coven who had been nodding respectfully as their priestess described their creed, now looked expectantly at Brother Richard. He paused for a while gathering his thoughts. Then he spoke.

"I can see that you are sincere people, but what you have described to me, as I understand it, is outside my experience and at odds with Catholic teaching. You will perhaps understand my difficulty in knowing how to proceed. What exactly is it you wish to discuss with regard to midsummer?"

In answer to this question Holly Garden, explained calmly:

"Brother Richard, Dalmannoch has been abandoned by the Catholic church for many years. It is a secluded spot and on the hillside behind this building is a spring; a holy well in medieval times but originally a sacred druidic site. For that reason Dalmannoch is sacred to us. Three years ago we approached Alexander Agnew,

121

whose murdered body I believe you found. We asked him if we could use the chapel here for our rituals and initiations on the understanding that we would keep it clean and in good condition. He saw the benefit in us acting as responsible custodians when the building may otherwise have fallen into ruin and had a key made for us. We have made periodic use of the chapel ever since. The last occasion was our celebration of Beltane or what others would call Mayday."

For the first time during this encounter, Brother Richard smiled.

"That explains a minor mystery Holly. I found a bus ticket dated the first of May in the chapel."

"So that's where I lost it", exclaimed Suzie Silver. "That was the return half of my ticket to Newton Stewart. I had to pay again for the return journey."

Brother Richard rummaged in a drawer and produced the ticket.

"Here you are Suzie. I don't know if it is still valid but there is no need for me to keep it now."

The smiling blond woman thanked the monk, saying that she would keep it as a souvenir and Holly rejoined her discourse.

"We became aware that, after all the years of neglect, things were stirring at Dalmannoch and that you had arrived to renovate the buildings. This is a worry to us and we wonder how we are placed regarding our future activities here and in particular our plans for our midsummer rites."

Brother Richard was in a quandary. How could he reconcile Pagan worship with a Catholic religious establishment for which he was responsible? He was sure Prior John would be horrified. After considering this, he spoke.

"This places me in a difficult position. I will need time to consider the best course of action. I will, however, treat your – em – request seriously and we'll see what might be possible. Now if you would let me know how I can contact you, I will be back in touch."

Holly Garden rose and handed Brother Richard a black card emblazoned with a silver Elven star. The others also rose, shook hands with Brother Richard and Frances. Thomas Nutter, the last to do so thanked the pair for listening and the Pagans made their departure in their extraordinary Kombi.

"Well," said Brother Richard, "what did you make of that?"

Frances pondered for a moment and declared:

"You know Richard, I rather liked them."

O N THE AFTERNOON of that same Friday, after the departure of the Pagans, Frances and Brother Richard prepared to set off for town to buy in materials and equipment for the weekend work party.

"For one thing we need carpet shampoo and a good heavy duty vacuum cleaner;" Frances stated firmly, "the carpets are filthy."

Brother Richard concurred and, as there was no telephone line to Dalmannoch, he asked:

"Can you get the lawyers on your mobile to confirm that an account has been set up at the builders' merchant? And I'll need an imprest for, say, £500 to keep us going in incidentals."

After trying the number, Frances shrugged: "I can't get a signal here. We'll need to get out onto the road before I can make contact."

With that they set off in the van, duly confirmed that accounts had been set up at the main suppliers, and that cash would be available against Brother Richard's signature at Agnew, Douglas and McWhirter's reception. After picking up the cash, they headed for the builders' merchant and loaded up with paint, brushes, rollers, masking tape, cleaning fluids and other requirements, including the vacuum cleaner, for the next stage of the Dalmannoch renovation. On the return journey a stop was made at the supermarket for the week's groceries.

Back at Dalmannoch as the evening meal was in preparation, Douglas Gordon appeared at the front door.

"Just checking that everything's on track for tomorrow and Sunday. We've rustled together eight or nine of us and we'll bring food and drink. Is that still OK?"

Brother Richard confirmed that indeed it was and that all would be welcome, in response to which Douglas asked:

"Some of us were wondering – well could we camp here over Saturday night? The weather forecast's good and it would mean we could have a wee drink in the evening – and not drive home that night."

Although not quite understanding the full significance of the request, Brother Richard agreed that he saw no objection to the suggested course of action. On receipt of this confirmation, Douglas Gordon departed.

* * *

At twenty to ten on Saturday morning the silver Peugeot hatch-back that had taken Douglas and Gordon on their first visit to Dalmannoch drew up by the front door. The driver and front passenger doors opened and from the one stepped the lugubrious Gordon and from the other Suzie Silver, still stunning looking but now dressed in short shorts and tee-shirt.

"Good morning Brother Richard, I believe you have already met Suzie. She's a member of our GGG."

"Yes indeed, Welcome again to Dalmannoch."

From the back of the car, clutching plastic carrier bags, came Douglas, accompanied by another eye-catching young woman.

"This is Trish McLellan, my fiancée", declared Douglas

"I'm very pleased to meet you and welcome. Come inside and we can work out our plan of campaign. But first a cup of tea I think – ah, here's Frances."

More introductions, tea, coffee and scones were followed by a succession of arrivals: firstly a middle aged man with silver hair and moustache accompanied by two ladies of indeterminate age and cases of bottles and cans.

"Good morning I'm Ronald Radcliff and may I introduce Ellen Crawford and Sophie Hamilton."

Next, a young man arrived, Iain Stewart by name, carrying a guitar, followed a few minutes later by a young couple Angus and Fiona Martin respectively carrying an accordion and a fiddle case.

As the group assembled Brother Richard was bemused as instruments, food parcels and boxes were deposited in the kitchen and Gaelic greetings were exchanged:

"Math d'fhaicinn. Ciamar a tha thu?"

"O, chan eil dona. Tha thu fhein gu math? . . ."[*]

"Well I found Wullie at the recycling centre difficult to follow," admitted Brother Richard, "but this is totally incomprehensible."

Trish McLellan explained that, while Wullie, and many others in Galloway, spoke Scots, a somewhat modified descendent of the language of the Northumbrians and closely related to English; Gaelic as a Celtic language was as different from English as, say, Greek. She continued:

"I hope you don't mind but we would like to practice our Gaelic as we work about the place. It helps us get the idioms into our heads. We're all learners you see."

---

[*] Gaelic translated as "Good to see you. How are you?" "Not bad, You're well yourself?"

Brother Richard, in anticipation of the inroads such a large group could make on transforming Dalmannoch, readily agreed to this request.

Frances, on the other hand, was listening intently to the ebb and flow of the language and was surprised that, she could understand some, but not all, of what was being said. This Scots Gaelic was as though she was listening to her own native Donegal Irish Gaelic on a badly tuned radio.

After an outline by Brother Richard as to what was required, the group set too with gusto, scraping wallpaper, sanding, filling, painting ceilings, staining and varnishing dados and skirtings, shampooing, polishing, cleaning, vacuuming while Gordon clambered about the kitchen, loft and under the floor checking pipes, fittings and lagging.

Around one o' clock, during a pause for a snack lunch and tea, coffee or juice, a new arrival appeared. This was the Reverend Donald Angus MacLeod, the group's teacher. He stepped out of a grey car of nondescript Far Eastern make, but what his car lacked in presence, he himself, made up for in spades. Although of no great age, he had a shock of black, slightly greying hair and beard, a winning smile and a set of bagpipes under his arm. He held out his hand.

"Brother Richard, I have heard a good deal about you – all good I may say. I'm very pleased to meet you at last."

"And I you, Reverend MacLeod. Come inside; there's tea and vittles on the go. I'm looking forward to having a chat with you."

"Please call me Donald, we don't stand on ceremony in the Gaelic Ulpan group or the GGG as we call it."

In conversation over tea and sandwiches, although the Reverend MacLeod was of a more ebullient disposition than Brother Richard, the two men found that they had much in common. He had been brought up on a croft in a Gaelic speaking community in the Isle of Skye and knew no English until he had gone to school. Like many others of his race, he did well at school, mastering English, Latin and French. On leaving school, like many islanders, he had gone to sea for some years before he got the call to the ministry. As his story unfolded, his speech had that same soft lilt and cadence that Brother Richard had heard among those of his former shipmates who had also hailed from one or other of the islands of the Hebrides.

The lunch-break lasted not half an hour and work activity resumed to the sound of Gaelic instructions, advice and banter. Brother Richard offered to show his fellow man of God round Dalmannoch and when they came to the chapel; its effect was as powerful as it had been with Professor Macdonald and Jamie Arbuckle.

"Quite amazing!" declared the minister, "I've never seen anything like it before – and so much more ornate than we are used to in the Church of Scotland.."

There is a range of out buildings at the rear of the main building. Brother Richard had been poking about them in the previous few of days. He took Donald thence to show him some elderly implements he had come across.

"Oh ho, a scythe," Donald Angus took hold of it, "the very thing to cut that wilderness of grass at the front. Have you ever used one of these things?"

Brother Richard confessed that he had not, at which his new companion volunteered to show him the technique.

"There's a knack to it, but we'll need to sharpen the blade first", explained the minister, who rummaged among the assortment of old implements and tools. He found a whinstone and proceeded to stroke the rusty scythe blade in a steady expert rhythm until its edge was razor sharp. Giving a fair impression of a younger version of Old Father Time, the Reverend Donald Angus MacLeod carried the implement to the overgrown front sward and commenced the cutting process with a steady swinging motion and a – swish – swish – as the vegetation fell away before him.

"This brings me back to my youth on the croft. I haven't done this for years. Now you have a go."

Brother Richard picked up the awkward frame as instructed and started to heave. The blade dug into the ground and stopped.

"No, don't push; just let the weight of the scythe do the work." Donald's words were calm, good humoured and encouraging. "That's it. You've got it."

For the next hour and a half on that warm sunny afternoon, monk and minister took turns at the scythe until a very respectable lawn had been created to set off the frontage of Dalmannoch's accommodation building and chapel.

HO RO GHEALLAIDH[*]

BETWEEN FOUR AND SIX, the focus of the work party changed. Douglas, Trish and Gordon appeared with rakes to help Donald clear away the cut vegetation into a big pile at the far end of the lawn; Ellen and Sophie took over the kitchen with Frances in attendance to prepare food; Ronald and Angus worked with Brother Richard to rip up some of the old window shuttering to create a long trestle table and construct makeshift benches. Only Iain and Suzie remained on painting duty tidying up edges and corners.

As all this was going on, a big green Volvo V70 Estate pulled up among the parked vehicles. It was Professor Ruairidh Alasdair Macdonald. He walked towards the front door clutching a bottle of malt whisky and a long parcel wrapped in newspaper and announced:

"I heard you were having a get together and couldn't resist coming. Left Inverness at midday. Here's a salmon my cousin – er – came across yesterday. My wife cooked it last night."

"Wonderful to see you Ruairidh," Brother Richard was genuinely pleased that his friend, of two weeks before, had turned up again, "And thanks very much for the whisky and the salmon. Let's take them through to the kitchen. It looks as though we're going to have a banquet."

The professor inspected the progress made with the renovation of the building since he had last seen it in its former dilapidated state and was impressed. He was

---

[*] Gaelic pronounced Ho ro <u>Ya</u>llee, meaning a soiree or party

introduced to Frances and was enchanted. Several of the others he already knew and, with those he did not, he soon became acquainted.

In due course the long table was erected on the newly cut lawn and set with plastic cutlery, paper plates (there were insufficient proper utensils in the as yet sparsely equipped kitchen) and glasses, which had been hired from a licensed grocer. It was thereafter laden with a copious variety food, bottles of wine, jugs of juice and water.

The eager company climbed or wriggled their way onto the crude but sturdy benches laid out on either side of the table. The early evening was still warm and a scent of myrtle mixed with the smell of cut grass and cooked food stimulated the senses, especially the taste-buds. The same cock blackbird that Brother Richard had heard on his first fateful arrival at Dalmannoch sang from the gable of the chapel and he felt that God was in his heaven and all was well with the world.

Brother Richard said a few words of grace – in Latin – just to provide some linguistic variety to this largely Gaelic occasion and the eating and drinking commenced.

As may be expected, the crack (amiable conversation) was excellent, aided by the wine; shrieks of laughter emanated from one end of the table at some, no doubt indecorous, Gaelic joke. Brother Richard and Frances sat opposite the professor and brought him up to date with all that had happened over the previous two weeks.

"Well Richard, you and Frances certainly have been busy and I have to admit, I'm amazed at how you have transformed the place. You know, now that I see it again and with a bit of redecoration, it would make an

131

excellent study centre for the kind of work I have been involved with here."

"Mm. It's interesting that you should say that Ruairidh," mulled Brother Richard, "because, Douglas and Gordon asked to use it *pro tem* as a place to hold their Gaelic meetings. I agreed, for as long as I am around, in exchange for the excellent work they have done today. I think I may have got the best of the bargain."

The Reverend MacLeod who was sitting next to the professor added:

"We're pretty pleased with the arrangement, and you know we have been speaking Gaelic all day. Using a language in a practical situation is far better than a formal class situation to hammer home idiom and useful phrases. That's how we learn as children. Truth to tell, I'm very impressed with how our little group has come on in its fluency."

When the meal was over and as the debris was being cleared away and tents erected on the lawn, the Reverend Donald stood on the lawn edge and played on his pipes a set of what to Brother Richard's ear was among the most haunting music he had ever heard. The sound seemed to infuse the space between the wood and the buildings with a strange magical calming ambience. Then when the tempo changed to March time, a more expectant mood pervaded and everyone repaired to the common room.

It seemed to go without saying that The Reverend Donald should be master of ceremonies, or 'fear an taighe' in Gaelic. Like some magician he coaxed each individual into performing.

Douglas gave a solo tenor rendition of 'Sìne Bhàn', a love song about a soldier's longing to return to his beloved young maiden. The company joined the chorus:

> Blath nan cailean Sìne Bhàn,
> Reul nan nighean dileas òg;
> Cuspair diomhair I do'm' dhàn,
> Gràdh mo chridh' an ribhin òg.

There were a couple more party pieces of this kind. Then the fear an taighe pulled the musicians together, had a quiet word with them and;

"Now take your partners for a 'Strip the Willow'. We need a set of eight now. Frances, a ghràidh, pull Richard onto the floor, its time he worked up a bit of a sweat!"

Richard was reluctant to participate in some unknown dance, but Frances urged and pulled him.

"It's great fun and not hard, I've danced this one in Donegal when we had a group of Highland students over on a cultural exchange. We can let Suzie and Gordon lead and we can go after Pat and Douglas. You'll soon get the hang of it."

Reluctantly the monk joined the set, while Ronald and Ellen took up bottom position.

"Just watch Gordon and Douglas and you do the same when it's your turn.

The music started, Gordon and Suzie linked arms and spun each other then Suzie 'striped' down the line of men alternatly swinging with Gordon. At the bottom, the couple joined again and spun, then Gordon 'striped' up the line of ladies altenating with Suzie. At the top of the set, the couple joined and spun together then 'striped', alternately swinging each other and the others' partners down the line to meet at the bottom for a last spin of eight beats. Then Douglas and Pat started the process all over. The pace was furious and when it was Richard and Frances turn, Frances spun Richard ferociously and guided him to swing her as she alternately swung the men down the line. On reaching the end of the line Richard swung alternately with the ladies and Frances up the line whence they alternately swung with each other and the respective ladies and men down again.

Brother Richard was relieved to reach the bottom without too many wrong moves only to realise the process was staring all over, with Suzie, then Pat spining him until he and Frances commenced another 'strip' down the line. At the end Brother Richard was panting for breath but giggling with joy.

Amid an enthusiastic round of applause for his efforts, and most enthusiastically of all by Frances, the now dishevelled monk gasped:

"That was amazing."

There was a pause to allow participants to catch breath, then Frances, who had all day been listening intently to the Gaelic spoken by the group, and seeking help with the differences between it and her Donegal Irish, was asked to sing.

In response she stood and explained that the song she was about to sing was called in Irish, 'Tá mé mo Shuí', which translated as 'I'm Sitting' a traditional song about the ache of true love. Her lilting voice sang slow and sweet:

> Casadh bean-tsí dom thíos ag Lios Bhéal an Átha
> Is d'fhiafraigh mé díthe an scaoilfeadh glas ar bith grá
> Is é dúirt sí os íseal i mbriathra soineannta sáimh

"Nuair a théann sé fán chroí cha scaoiltear as é go bráth."

The beauty of Frances voice, her poise and the power of the emotion she expressed, moistened the eyes of most in that gathering. Not least of these was Brother Richard. Even although he could not understand the words of her song, he realised that he was in love with this wonderful Irish woman.

THE MORNING AFTER THE NIGHT BEFORE

THE CÈILIDH[*] had gone on until the wee small hours when couples had started pairing off. A little before midnight, the Reverend MacLeod had made a tactful exit. The professor, Ronald, Ellen and Sophie had also departed a couple of hours later. The others of the Galloway Gaelic Group had merely slipped out to the lawn and into their tents.

"Oo my head", said Frances in the morning as she came down for breakfast; "Great night but too much wine and whisky mixed together. How are you my lovely dancing monk?"

Brother Richard had been up for some time. He looked at her. His feelings of the previous night were undiminished. He sighed:

"I fear my monking days may be drawing to a close. I'm straying too far from the straight monastic path."

There were a few moments silence and then Frances said, "That's a big announcement Richard. Do you want to talk about it?"

There was another pause and then:

"I do – yes I do very much, but not right now. I'll be going over to St Aidan's in a little while. Perhaps when I come back and after the others have gone, I'll tell you what's on my mind."

Frances was in a turmoil of curiosity, hope and apprehension as to what this notion might mean, but

---

[*] Cèilidh: Gaelic, pronounced Kae̱lee, literally meaning a visit, but nowadays understood as a participative event featuring musical and other traditional entertainment.

decided to let things be. Richard clearly needed time to sort his mind out and she realised it was only fair to give him that time. She changed the subject.

"Any sign of the campers yet?"

"Yes, there have been a few back and forward to the bathroom," the troubled monk replied. "I expect they'll be along for breakfast soon."

And so it transpired. One by one and two by two the campers assembled in the kitchen for a Sunday breakfast of porridge, orange juice, bacon and eggs, toast, marmalade and tea or coffee as dietary preferences determined. The conversation was somewhat more subdued than on the previous evening, but all seemed happy with the progress made with the renovations and with the memory of the ho ro gheallaidh.

"That was a grand night last night," said Douglas. "This place would be great for us to meet regularly. What plans do you have for Dalmannoch once you have finished the renovations?"

"Well," replied Brother Richard, "I don't really know what the future holds. The trust that owns it is looking for a buyer. Someone that will maintain the spiritual purpose of the place. Goodness knows where such a buyer could be found."

"Och, if only I was stinking rich," sighed Douglas, "I'd buy it and turn it into a Gaelic centre, and we could have regular hoolies[*] like we had last night."

"Oh Aye Duggie," echoed Gordon, "that'd be just dandy, but I doot there's nae chance o us finding that kin o siller. Whit wid it cost – a million pun'?"

"I confess, I really don't know what the value would be," admitted Brother Richard. "And speaking of

_____

[*] Hoolie: a Scots word meaning a rumpus or party.

137

confession, I'm heading off to St Aidan's now. I'll be back later and meantime Frances will look after you."

Frances walked with him to the van and, after a kiss and a little cuddle, consoled: "Things will work out Richard. I know they will." And with that the monk started up the old van and departed.

Back in the kitchen Frances re-joined the members of the Galloway Gaelic Group.

"You know," said Suzie, "I feel this place gives off an ambience of harmony. I know it has been run-down and neglected but after yesterday's efforts it's looking brighter. I can see with a bit of artistic flair in its redecoration it could be really special. Can we not find some way of taking it on for the GGG and – well – other groups who would appreciate it?"

Suzie's physical loveliness and demeanour may have, at first sight, suggested a kind of fey empty-headedness; now her hidden artistic and practical depths were beginning to emerge. Notwithstanding her Pagan leanings she was in an apparently healthy relationship with the quiet unassuming practical Gordon, who, through his flourishing business as a plumber, was the highest earning member of the GGG.

"I agree with you Suzie", concurred Frances. "This place has great potential." I'm growing fond of it myself. It would be good to find a way of turning it into something worthwhile – but . . ."

Trish McLellan, who had been listening to the debate while leaning against the work top screwed up her face with thought and ventured: "Couldn't we set up a new trust Duggie, or something to take the place over?

Douglas, who was an accountant by profession and cautious by nature, put his arm round her shoulder and sighed: "It would be great my love, but where would the money come from?"

The answer to that question was not forthcoming.

"Enough of this speculation for now," enjoined Frances. "Let's make ourselves useful. I suggest we dismantle the long table on the lawn and put it up in sections in the dining room."

This suggestion was acted upon. The long table that had been assembled hurriedly for the previous evening's al fresco meal had been made in sections from the timber that had boarded up the building while out of use. The benches and trestles had likewise been assembled from this material. Such had been Brother Richard's ingenuity in construction that it was a relatively simple matter to separate the main components, move them to the dining room and reassemble them there, as three separate tables with sitting benches on either side of each.

"It's not the Ritz", said Frances, "but now at least we have somewhere where more than a handful people can sit down to eat."

A light lunch was prepared and consumed in the dining room, with its newly made crude but tolerable furniture.

No one felt like doing much work after that. Some sat around reading or simply lazing. Frances joined Gordon, Suzie and Iain to stroll up the slope at the back of the buildings, to see the little spring overhung by birch and alder trees. Suzie acted as guide, for she had been there many times before. From tree branches around the spring hung a few strips of rotting cloth.

"Who put the cloth there", asked Iain.

"I don't know who," said Suzie, "but I know why. Pieces of cloth are dipped in the water by those seeking healing and then tied to a branch while a prayer of supplication is said to the spirit of the well. Christians may pray to a saint; Pagans pray to the nature spirit. It's a continuation of the ancient Celtic practice of leaving votive offerings. This spring is called St Madrine's Well. The church made Madrine or Madrun a saint but she was really a pre-Christian Celtic goddess."

All present could not but be impressed by this unusual young woman's insights into Celtic lore.

When the strollers returned, Brother Richard had reappeared and the company prepared to leave. Thanks were exchanged, on the one hand, for the work done and, on the other, for the anticipated use of the building by the GGG. To the accompaniment of farewells in English, Scots and Gaelic, cars were started and, one by one, they departed, leaving Richard and Frances alone.

* * *

"They're lovely people but I'm glad we have the place to ourselves again", admitted Frances.

"Me too", said the monk.

The pair of them walked in silence holding hands and enjoying the afternoon sun. As they rounded the perimeter of the lawn to the rough grass by the edge of the wood, a startled wood pigeon fluttered. After a while Brother Richard spoke.

"I had a talk with Father McGuire today." Brother Richard paused, then spoke again. "I'm a monk in the stages of postulancy. In a couple of years or so, I'm supposed to take my Solemn Vows to commit fully to the monastic life." He paused again. "The thing is Frances;" he paused. "That path is at odds with my feelings for you. The fact is Frances, I love you."

Frances looked at him with soft eyes and quivering lip.

"I'm glad, for I love you with all my heart."

They embraced and kissed the deepest and sweetest of kisses, sank to the soft shaded ground still in each others' arms.

A NEW DAWN FOR DALMANNOCH

T WO DAYS AFTER the Galloway Gaelic Group had gone home, Hector Woodrow-Douglas called to see how the renovation work had progressed. On hearing about the substantial contribution made by the GGG and about the cèilidh and sleep-over, he was heartened, particularly so after inspecting the amount of actual work done.

"Its preparation work mainly," said Brother Richard, "but Frances and I were just discussing what we should do about decoration."

Frances added: "One of the members of the Gaelic group – Suzie Silver – has some very imaginative ideas for the interior."

"That sounds real interesting," Hector consented in his deliberate Canadian way, "but hold your horses. Don't let's move ahead of ourselves."

Frances and Brother Richard looked at each other, wondering what was in the Canadian businessman's mind. He explained:

"Since we last met, in fact even before that, I have been mulling over some ideas about keeping Dalmannoch out of that Edward North guy's clutches; maybe setting up a new legal structure to take the place over. The thing is I have made my pile in Canada. I'm semi-retired; my son is more or less running the show there and I'd like to stake a claim back here in Scotland. Don't get me wrong, I have a good life in BC (British Columbia, that is), but I'd like a place where I could lay my head from time to time – a place here with a family connection. To cut to the chase, I like how you have tackled the renovation work here and I'd be interested to invest in Dalmannoch – not as sole stakeholder, but as a partner – with another or others who would have a real stake in caring for it and making it work as a viable operation."

"Well!" said Brother Richard.

"Well, well, well!" said Frances. "You know Hector, the Gaelic group were just talking about how good it would be to find a way of taking on Dalmannoch as a kind of cultural centre where they could hold their meetings and events and such like. They don't have any money, but they have energy; we can both vouch for that."

"We can indeed", assured Brother Richard, adding, "And there was another group asking about using the place – a kind of spiritual Pagan bunch."

"That's interesting – yes it sure is," deliberated Hector, "But what I was wondering was this: Would you both be prepared to stay on here as managers?"

There was a pause as Frances looked at Richard and then hesitatingly ventured:

"Oh Richard, why don't we?"

Richard stroked his chin.

"For me it's not quite so straight forward, but . . . mm . . . There's something to be said for it . . . I'll need to think about it."

Frances chipped in; "How much is this place worth?"

"That's a good question, Frances," affirmed Hector, "Catriona Macarthur reckons, bearing in mind the restrictions imposed by the trust deed, it could fetch say five to seven hundred thousand pounds on a good day."

"Well, as it happens," ventured Frances, "I have a couple of hundred thousand, I need to find a home for,

for a few years. I'd consider putting a good whack of that in the pot so long as I could get it back eventually."

Hector whistled: "Now that IS interesting. It looks as though we could have the bones of a deal."

"So, if it can all be pulled together," queried Brother Richard, "and it's a big 'if', what are the next steps?"

"The next step is a coffee for Hector and tea for you Richard", interjected Frances; "unless you want something stronger? We have booze left over from the cèilidh."

"No, no, coffee will be fine", confirmed Hector holding up his hand in mock protest.

While Frances was in the kitchen boiling the kettle, Professor Macdonald's green Volvo arrived and the ebullient academic joined the company with a:

"Hope I'm not butting in."

"By no means Ruairidh, welcome back," confirmed Brother Richard; "we're just about to have tea – tea, coffee, whisky?" On ascertaining the professor's preference, the monk shouted through to the kitchen: "One more coffee Frances", then introduced the professor to the businessman.

"Professor Macdonald has taken an interest in our work at Dalmannoch. He encouraged the Galloway Gaelic Group to help us; I think it would be useful, with your agreement Hector, to enlighten him as to your thoughts for the future."

This was agreed and Hector outlined his idea of setting up a new legal structure, with multiple stakeholders, to buy Dalmannoch and to operate it as an, as yet undefined, spiritual cum cultural centre.

The professor pondered: "I would need to consider the detail, but in principle, it seems to me that your ideas have merit. If it helps the case, I could do with a base here to develop my own research work which is aided by the Galloway Gaelic Group. I have links too with Universities in Ireland, Wales, Canada and the US, so it may be possible to build up an international customer base with an interest in Celtic numinosity."

"Numinosity?" echoed Hector and Frances.

"Numinosity – oh," explained the professor, "it's from 'numinous' meaning power or presence of a divinity, or belief in the sacred, the holy, and the transcendent. It's an area of study that interests me, particulatly the relationship between the Pagan Celts and the early Christian Church."

"Well, well, Ruairidh, you son of a gun," exclaimed Hector, "you would have got on like a house on fire with my great grandfather. He was into all that stuff. He founded the chapel here at Dalmannoch."

"Well did he now?" retorted the professor, whereupon Hector outlined the antiquarian interests and activities of his ancestor, Sir Joseph Douglas, who had gifted the land on which the Dalmannoch chapel and retreat was built. The two men had clearly found a common interest that could have been expanded upon, were it not for the ever practical Brother Richard bringing them back to the matter at issue.

"This is all fascinating and will be food for much consideration if we can get Dalmannoch operating along the lines you have in mind, but if we are to achieve that end, what action do we have to take?"

"Well done Richard," agreed Hector; "back to business. Firstly we will need a plan setting out the why, who and how of the enterprise – a business plan so to speak. Then we will have to create a new legal entity, and after that we will have to affect the transfer of the property. Now as Agnew, Douglas and McWhirter have a trustee on the existing Damnannoch Trust, they will handle the sale. We will need a separate legal firm to deal with the purchase and presumably with the creation of the new entity. That's it in a nutshell."

"When you put it like that," said Brother Richard, "it sounds simple enough. I dare say there's a bit more to it, but we might as well make a start. I have to say that Catriona Macarthur has served us very well so far, but if we need a separate lawyer, I have met a Robert Heron who has a practice in Newton Stewart and who has at least heard of Dalmannoch. Indeed, if I recall, he offered his services should we need them. Why don't we make contact and call to see him – or invite him here?

"Richard, for someone who has been here for less than three weeks," exclaimed Ruairidh, "you are remarkably well connected."

Brother Richard shrugged: "An awful lot has happened. It seems like I've been here for months. In fact I met Robert Heron before I even arrived here."

It was agreed that contact would be made with Robert Heron and a preliminary meeting convened.

The professor then turned to Brother Richard saying: "This has all been most stimulating, but I had another reason for visiting you. My wife was to join me for this trip, but her younger sister has just had a baby and she has stayed behind to help out. I have two tickets for a special cruise to the Isle of Man on Saturday from Garlieston in the Machars here. I have to meet with a contact there but Fiona's ticket's going a begging and I just wondered if you fancied joining me for the trip."

"Mm – sounds too good to pass up", said Brother Richard.

"Oo could I come too?" asked Frances.

"I'm sure you can still get tickets. I'll make enquiries tonight," confirmed the professor. And with that he and Hector went their separate ways.

DESPITE THE MIST on the Saturday morning, Frances was very excited about the Isle of Man trip. She and Brother Richard arrived at the little Machars port of Garlieston at eight o clock, a good hour before sailing time. They parked Frances' Renault in one of the village's back streets called Cowgate and, armed with plastic bags of sandwiches and cold drinks, they ambled towards the pier, alongside which lay *Balmoral* a small smart traditional black hulled, white funnelled passenger ship.

On reaching the pier a fair crowd had already assembled and among those present, as had been pre-arranged, was Professor Ruairidh Macdonald.

"Here are the vouchers for the tickets", announced the professor. Sailing time is nine o' clock so we have stacks of time, but we might as well go aboard."

The tide was in and *Balmoral* rode high in the water, such that the gangway to the shelter deck lay at quite a steep angle. At the bottom of the gangway, vouchers were checked by the uniformed purser and the three of them climbed aboard. Brother Richard was intrigued by this classic motor-ship and the three immediately set out to explore. They noted from the builder's plate that *Balmoral* was built in Southampton by J I Thornycroft in 1949. She was well appointed with lounges, bar, dining saloon and a shop selling books and souvenirs.

"This is like stepping back in time, isn't it," suggested Frances; "I wouldn't be surprised if Hercule Poirot was on board with a host of suspicious characters."

"Oh no ! Please," protested Brother Richard with a grin, "one murder is quite enough to be going on with thank you very much Miss Gruesome."

"Come on you pair," urged the professor, "the ship's filling up. Let's find a good perch on deck for'ard so that we can see what there is to see."

A slatted wooden seat was selected on the fore-deck and in due course the tinkling of the engine-room telegraph announced that Balmoral was about to depart. A low rumble from the nether regions prompted Brother Richard to join a group of mainly men and boys leaning on the rail to watch the bow line being slackened and then cast off and wound inboard by a sailor operating the fo'csle windlass. The good ship was under way.

She proceeded astern in an arc into Wigtown Bay, then the telegraph signalled stop, then half ahead, then full ahead and *Balmoral* surged onto her southerly course down the rugged east coat of the Machars peninsula.

The mist had cleared sufficiently for the main coastal features to be identified to starboard by the professor.

"That arched ruin on the edge of the cliff there is Cruggleton Castle. It dates from the twelfth century and was occupied by the Lords of Galloway, the Earls of Buchan, the Douglas family and the Prior of Whithorn among others until it was abandoned in the seventeenth century."

Balmoral ploughed on southwards and quarter of an hour later he pointed:

"Look, we're passing Isle of Whithorn now. There's the little promontory with the white cube where you and I first met Richard. Now we're coming into the open Irish Sea. Pity it's so hazy. We'll not see the Isle of

Man until we get much closer even although this is the nearest point in the UK to the island."

Once out of site of land, Richard, who was thoroughly enjoying being afloat again, decided to take a stroll round the ship. By a companion-way he went below to check out the main lounge and the dining saloon. As he entered the latter, he heard a:

"Hello Brother Richard, fancy meeting you on board." It was Catriona Macarthur, sitting at a table with a coffee in the company of Robert Heron and Betty MacDowell.

"Good morning Miss Macarthur, Robert, Betty", the monk responded. "What a pleasant surprise."

"Half the population of the Machars is on board today," Robert declared. "Come, join us for a coffee. I hear you have interesting plans for Dalmannoch. Hector Woodrow-Douglas came to see Catriona and me on Thursday – separately, that is, but let's not talk business. We will arrange a meeting of the interested parties next week."

Brother Richard joined the little group for a while and then made his excuses to return to Frances and Ruairidh. On the way back on deck, he noticed that there were indeed a number of faces he recognised from local shops, and from Alexander Agnew's funeral.

A little later a red and white striped lighthouse emerged out of the haze.

"Ah," proclaimed the professor, "that's Point of Ayre lighthouse – the most northerly point of the Isle of Man. We'll be passing the town of Ramsey in less than half an hour."

Richard noted that, from what he could make out, the island was quite low lying, an impression that was soon dispelled as the mist cleared and the little ship passed what the professor identified as Maughold Head. Here the coast was even more rugged than that of the Machars. Behind Maughold Head was a range of mountains with a particularly prominent conical eminence in the foreground.

"That's North Barrule," announced the professor and behind with clouds on the top is Snaefell – the highest peak on the island. Do you know that from its top, on a clear day, you can see seven kingdoms?" There was a twinkle in the professor's eye and those of Frances.

Brother Richard thought for a bit.

"You're pulling my leg."

"Not at all," said the professor, "They are: the kingdoms of Scotland, England Wales, Ireland and Mann – plus Neptune's Kingdom – and – the Kingdom of Heaven."

"Ho, ho," exclaimed the monk, "very clever. But surely Mann is not a kingdom."

"Oh, indeed it is," the professor protested, "the Kingdom of Mann and The Isles was a powerful independent realm until the thirteenth century when it was ceded by Norway to the Kings of Scots and later to England. The Isle of Man has never been part of the United Kingdom and is to all intents an independent state with its own laws and taxes. Like other Commonwealth countries, the Queen is head of state but she is known here as Lord of Mann."

"Well, well, fancy that", said Brother Richard, "we live and learn. I'm beginning to wonder if there is anything you don't know about these parts."

"I couldn't possibly say", quipped the academic. Frances joined in:

"OK boys, while you two are bantering, I suggest we eat our grub now so that we have as much time as possible to explore when we get there." Frances then unwrapped the little bundles of sandwiches – egg and tomato – ham – cheese. The sea air must have whetted their appetites, for the entire provision was consumed there and then.

Between mouthfuls and swigs of juice, the professor drew attention to various points of interest. "That's the village of Laxey with its famous waterwheel, the world's biggest, designed to pump water from the Glen Mooar lead mine. The mine was two thousand feet deep; as deep as Snaefell is high."

A little later *Balmoral* swung round what the professor identified as Onchan Head and into a broad bay, nestled in which spread the island capital, Douglas bathed in sunshine. In another ten minutes, it was twelve o' clock and they were along-side a substantial pier. The ship's public address system announced a series of further excursions, including a cruise to the Calf of Man and reminded those going ashore, that the return departure would be at six o' clock sharp.

It took quarter of an hour before the trio passed through the Sea Terminal building. At its entrance stood a smiling gentleman dressed in blazer and light slacks; Juan[*] Corlett,

Member of the House of Keys, the Manx parliament, and long-standing friend of Ruairidh, whom he welcomed with a:

"Fastyr mie Ruairidh. Failt ort dys Mannin."

---

[*] Juan is the Manx rendering of John and is pronounced <u>Joo</u>an and NOT as Spanish Hwan

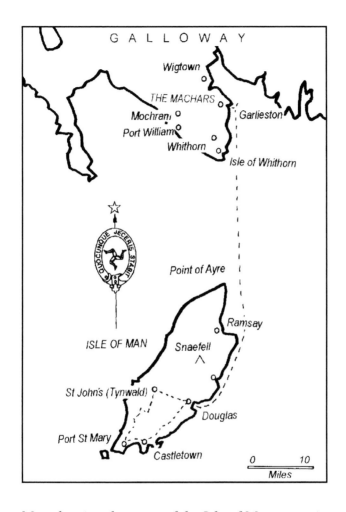

Map showing the route of the Isle of Man excursion

FRANCES WAS ALL SMILES as she, Brother Richard, Professor Macdonald and Juan Corlett MHK strolled in the warm sunshine along the Manx capital's Loch Promenade. This broad thoroughfare, edging Douglas Bay is characterised by its terraced, stuccoed hotels and boarding houses, horse drawn trams and myriad flag poles flying the red Manx flag charged with the three legs of Mann.

"This is just as I remember it as a child", declared Frances, delighted. "It feels like such a bright laid-back happy place."

"Yes," assented Juan Corlett; "I'd have to agree with you; the Isle of Man is a favoured isle. I wouldn't live anywhere else, no matter what you paid me. Ruairidh and I have a little work to do and have arranged a meeting with some Manx language people down in Port St Mary but you're all welcome to come along for the ride and see some of the sights."

The little group turned left into Regent Street, past the Manx Post Office, which Juan pointed out as being wholly independent of the Royal Mail and issuing its own attractive stamps. They then turned right into narrow Strand Street, in which are located Douglas' main shops. They soon reached the Lexicon Bookshop which, on account of its wide range of Manx books, Ruairidh couldn't resist entering for a browse, eventually selecting a number of books for purchase. As Brother Richard scanned the shelves, he was surprised to see such a large and varied assortment of books on wholly Manx topics.

"We'd better make tracks," chivvied Juan, "if we are going to get to Port St Mary – and back in time for your boat," and they passed through a lane to a lift and up into the Chester Street multi-storeyed car park where Juan's car was parked. Out of the car park they drove, down Finch Road past the white wedding-cake-like Government Building, seat of Tynwald, the Manx parliament, and along Atholl Street to the Peel Road.

Juan and Ruairidh sat in the front discussing the latest developments in reviving the Manx language while Frances and Richard sat in the back like two happy teenagers, oblivious of this exchange, but looking alternately at the lush rural scene and at each other. Twenty minutes later they reached a village with a tall steepled church, two lines of flagpoles and a curious tiered hillock surmounted by a flagpole from which flew a large red Manx flag. Juan stopped the car. They all got out and pointing, he announced:

"This is St John's and that is the Tynwald Hill. It's here on each 5th July that the two houses of the Manx parliament meet together at an open air ceremony to promulgate all the laws of the previous year. This has been going on for over a thousand years. In fact it's the world's oldest continuously operating parliament. It's quite a spectacle and of course a Manx national holiday. You must come back on Tynwald day and I'll get you a ringside seat."

Ruairidh had seen the site before and had indeed attended the ceremony as a guest of Juan. But Richard and Frances were fascinated to hear about the procession from St John's church along the rush-strewn avenue to the Tynwald hill where the combined House of Keys, Legislative Council, Leiutenent Governor, Deemsters and other dignatories sat to hear the names of the laws read in English and in Manx Gaelic and to receive

155

special petitions by anyone who may have some grievance or may seek a change in the law.

"And over there is our Manx language primary school, Bunscoill Ghaelgagh. Everything, is taught through the Manx language which we call Gaelg. It's similar to Scots Gaelic. The last of the old native speakers, Ned Maddrell, died in 1974, but the language never died and it has, in fact, undergone quite a revival in recent years and is considered an important part of the island's culture and heritage. The number of fluent speakers is still quite low but growing."

Juan continued:

"Ruairidh has been telling me about your group in Galloway trying to stimulate a revival of your Gaelic there. I think we have much to learn from each other, especially as your language is still quite strong in some Scottish communities."

"Well," responded Brother Richard, "it's hardly my language. Until a week ago, I knew nothing of Gaelic, but I have to say I did hear quite a bit last weekend and it's all a bit of a mystery to me – so far. But Frances speaks Irish Gaelic and she seems to be able to make sense of it."

"To some extent," confessed Frances. "But I think with a bit of work I could get a proper hang of it. I'd love to hear a bit of Manx though, to see if I could make something of that."

"Then that you shall", said Juan ushering the group back to the car. "Onwards to Port St Mary."

The car turned south and ever upwards past the former lead mining village of Foxdale, along the eastern flanks of what Juan indicated as the hills of Barrule Beg and South Barrule, through a forestry plantation, turning left on to a minor road that offered a superb prospect over the southern part of the island. To the left, beyond rolling farmland and small settlements, Juan pointed out the former island capital of Castletown, while some miles ahead lay Port Erin and Port St Mary.

At length they arrived at a pub called the 'Albert' in the latter place where a number of Manx language activists had forgathered to converse in their beloved Celtic tongue. Juan introduced Professor Macdonald, Brother Richard and Frances to the group and *vice versa*. Among the group was a dark haired woman, Fenella Qualtrough, a folklore and music specialist, whom the professor and MHK had arranged to meet. Pints of the first-rate Okells Manx bitter were ordered and in due course Juan, Ruairidh and Fenella removed themselves to a quiet corner to discuss their business. Meanwhile Frances had become the centre of attraction and a two way exchange, through a bizarre mixture of Manx and Irish Gaelic and English, commenced, on the one hand, as to her life story and on the other hand as to theirs. Much as she was in her element, Brother Richard felt a little left out and decided to take himself off to the nearby harbour.

There he met an old sailor, by the name of Finlo Cain, painting his small boat and, after a halting start; the two discovered a mutual interest in fishing lore.

"Ah yes," recalled Finlo in his soft Manx lilt, "in my grandfather's day there was hunthreds of boats sailin' out of here and Castletown and Peel. Away in the spring to the mackerel off Kinsale and then to the herrin' off Shetland in summer. Oh, they was exlen fast sailers them Nickies."

"Nickies? Brother Richard enquired.

157

"Nickies, that's what they called them, lug rigged; they say the design came from visitin' Cornish luggers an' Nicolas bein' a poplar Cornish name."

Well my name, before I became a monk was Nicolas, after my Cornish mother's brother. He fished out of Newlyn."

"Well, well, so you're a real Cornish Nickie." The old man was much amused and Brother Richard didn't have the heart to tell him that he actually hailed from Devon.

By half past four Juan and the professor rounded up the little group and set off back to Douglas, via Castletown for a quick view in the passing of Castle Rushen one of Europe's best preserved medieval castles and former seat of the Kings and Lords of Mann.

Frances felt very happy after the unusual and stimulating exchange with her new found Manx friends and Brother Richard likewise following his yarn with old Finlo. Ruairidh too was particularly pleased with his exchange with Fenella and some proposed joint fields of study.

"The Manx language activists are keen to explore working with us in Galloway and Dalmannoch may be the very place to make that happen."

When they reached Douglas, parked the car and made their way to the Sea Terminal, it was after half past five. A queue had formed ready for boarding *Balmoral*. Frances, Richard and Ruairidh joined the line and awaited the instruction to board for the return sailing. Then Frances gasped, grabbed Richard's arm and whispered:

"Look Richard, that man ahead with the rucksack; he's the man I saw arguing with Gerry in Merrion Square Park."

158

BROTHER RICHARD cast his eyes at the man pointed out by Frances. While the monk was by nature inclined to give individuals the benefit of any doubt as to their character, he found it difficult to empathise in the case of this particular individual. The sour expression, tattooed neck, shaved head and scar on his cheek presented a wholly unsavoury prospect. The large rucksack he carried seemed somehow out of place. He didn't look like the outdoor type.

"Let's try to keep our distance from him," Brother Richard recommended. "I don't suppose he'll recognise you but just in case, try to avoid eye contact with him and we'll avoid him as best we can once we're on board."

The queue began to move towards the gangway and by sailing time all were on board. The engine room telegraph tinkled, lines were cast off and *Balmoral* was once more under way. Brother Richard suggested making for the dining saloon as none of the trio had eaten anything substantial since their late morning sandwiches. Inevitably they were not alone in their aspiration and there was already quite a queue at the servery. A few places in front of them in the queue were Catriona Macarthur, Robert Heron and Betty MacDowell.

"Keep three places for us if you can," urged Brother Richard when he caught Catriona's eye and soon all six were seated at a port side window table viewing the passing Manx coast against a sun sparkled sea.

"What did you all do today?" enquired Brother Richard of the legal set.

"Oh we had a good time," answered Catriona. "We took a horse tram to the end of the prom and then an ancient 'toast-rack' electric tram to Laxey where we went up the water wheel and learnt all about the old lead and zinc mine. Do you know the miners had to go down two thousand feet on dark wet slippery ladders before they started to earn money AND they had to supply their own candles. It must have been a hard life for them. We didn't have time to go up Snaefell but we did get a chance to look round some of the shops when we got back to Douglas. And how did you get on?"

Frances described the excursion to Port St Mary and the general satisfaction felt by each in their own way and the professor mentioned a possible future role of Dalmannoch in brokering joint Gaelic studies between the Manx and Scots Gaelic activists.

"And Irish", added Frances

"Yes indeed," the professor acknowledged; "Frances was quite a hit with our Manx friends. Which reminds me; I must make contact with my Irish colleagues in Galway and Dublin to explore possible links with Irish academia."

"And," broke in Brother Richard, "we really must meet up next week with yourselves and Hector Woodrow Douglas to work out a way forward for Dalmannoch."

It was agreed that separate meetings would be held with Catriona and Robert on the following Tuesday to put in train the setting up of a new legal entity and the conveyance of Dalmannoch to the new body.

The conversation came to an end when Frances noticed that the unsavoury man, they had spotted earlier, had entered the dining saloon. Frances explained her desire to avoid this person and she and Richard left to go on deck.

Standing together at the taffrail, Richard and Frances watched the Point of Ayre Lighthouse and the Manx hills recede astern in the creaming wake while ahead lay Bonny Gallowa' with its protective backdrop of hills. The sea was calm and the westering sun made the sea sparkle and dance – an altogether idyllic scene spoilt only by the spectre of that rucksack carrying individual below.

"You know Richard, I'm sure he's up to no good. He just doesn't ring true as a back-packer. Do you think the rucksack could be loaded with drugs?

"Hmm, you may be right. What was it Inspector Morrison said? Gerry 'may have been pressed into the drugs business to pay off his debts'. And if Gerry was in discussion with this man, it may possibly have been about transporting drugs. I suppose this excursion would be a good way of avoiding the usual ports – I think we should contact the police. We could ask the ships radio operator to send a message ahead."

"Why not use the mobile phone?" suggested Frances.

"Ah, of course, I forgot. But the number – damn it – sorry – I've left the inspectors card at Dalmannoch. Look just dial 999."

This Frances did and the response came quickly. Frances replied:

"Police please . . . I'd like to report a suspected case of drug trafficking . . . Yes drug trafficking . . . My name is Frances McGarrigle . . . Dalmannoch, near Whithorn . . . Whithorn in Galloway . . . The man is a passenger on the *Balmoral* approaching Garlieston . . . no, a ship . . . Garlieston – G A R L I E S T O N . . . near Wigtown . . . Yes . . . No I'm on the *Balmoral* too with friends . . . We arrive at nine o' clock . . . No

161

tonight – in an hour's time . . . This is urgent. Inspector Morrison of, I believe, the Galloway Divisional Command, knows some of the background and asked us to let him know of such leads. You need to have someone at the pier when the ship arrives . . . Yes, he has a shaved head a tattoo on his neck and a scar on his cheek. He's wearing a blue waterproof jacket, navy trousers, white trainers and a large blue rucksack . . . No I don't know his name . . . Please hurry . . . Yes this number . . . Thank you."

Frances was trembling after the effort of conveying the required information to the doubting police officer.

"Well done love," Brother Richard comforted her, "you've done what you can. Let's hope they get to Garlieston in time. I think meantime we had better tell the master what we have done."

The monk then made his way to the purser's office and asked for an audience with the captain. This was arranged and master and monk toured the ship until the suspected drug trafficker was surreptitiously pointed out.

* * *

As *Balmoral* berthed at Garlieston, Brother Richard, Frances, Ruairidh, Catriona, Robert and Betty lined the foredeck to observe events. A police car was parked to the landward of, and just behind, the pier sheds. When the gangway was secured, the captain himself was first ashore, He spoke with the two officers who positioned themselves at the foot of the gangway and then re-boarded his ship.

162

The passengers were then asked to disembark. They streamed ashore and it was some time before the man with the rucksack proceeded down the gangway, his eyes avoiding the officers. The captain gave a signal. The officers stopped their suspect. A few words were exchanged. The man with the rucksack tried to bolt for it. He was floored within a ten yards, relieved of his rucksack, handcuffed and bundled into the police car.

As this was unfolding Betty noticed another man whom, she thought she recognised, and who had been watching the drama. Then she realised, shouting:

"That's the man Arbuckle; that's the man who called for Alec the day he was murdered!"

The man looked up. Frances looked down. Their eyes met. She gasped:

"That's my husband Gerry Flynn."

T HE CHIEF SUPERINTENDENT was perturbed that no real progress had been made in finding and arresting the killer of Alexander Agnew. Inspector Morrison pondered Brother Richard's suggestion that the murder could have some connection with Whitleigh and in the absence of any other option decided that there could be merit in a visit to the priory to gain some understanding of who may have had contact with whom.

As a starting point he called to see Catriona Macarthur at the offices of Agnew, Douglas and McWhirter. Miss Macarthur was open and helpful, but there was not much new data to go on.

"Alec carried so much information in his head," advised the young lawyer, "that he was not the most methodical of men in his filing. I have found a number of scribbled notes in his desk drawer. Here's one mentioning Edward North, with a phone number and the words 'Not appropriate !!!'. And then there is another one with the prior of Whitleigh Priory's phone number and 'phone Monday re visit of Br. R'."

"Not much to go on but it's at least something", admitted the inspector afterwards to the Chief Superintendent. "I suggest a visit to Whitleigh and a sniff around the area may be worth a shot." The Chief agreed to this course of action, contact was made with the local police and Inspector Morrison and Sergeant Watt headed south by car for the Cotswolds.

The local police booked them into the Fleece Hotel, in the centre of the Cotswold capital; Cirencester. It was a comfortable olde worlde establishment with ancient timber beams and private parking. They arrived that evening, had dinner, a nightcap and retired early.

Next morning they met with a Chief Inspector Davies, briefed him as to the nature of their enquiries and then set off for the picturesque Cotswold village of Wethercott St Giles and the nearby Whitleigh Priory for an appointment with the prior, Father John Ainslie.

After pleasantries, introductions, and a general description as to the broad circumstances of the murder, Inspector Morrison asked:

"Father Ainslie, could you tell us, so far as you know, who at Whitleigh knew about Dalmannoch and the project with which Brother Richard is involved?"

"Well yes – let me see – well, firstly there is myself of course. Our Bishop Wilfred Newman had first informed me of its existence about a year ago. He is one of the trustees of the Dalmannoch Trust, along with – er – the late Alexander Agnew, whom I met here with the bishop about three or four months ago and a Mr Woodrow-Douglas, a Canadian gentleman whom I have not met. Brother Richard was informed about my wish for him to go to Dalmannoch, if I recall some two weeks, or perhaps a little more, before he left and I had telephone conversations about his impending arrival with both the bishop and Mr Agnew a few days before he actually left.

Then there is Brother Jacob, our store master, I had briefed him on the project. It was his responsibility to equip Brother Richard with what he required in terms of a vehicle, tools and such like. Brother Jacob has many contacts. I have kept him informed on progress at Dalmannoch in case his services are required.

I also mentioned Dalmannoch in passing to our architect, Jamie Arbuckle on the basis that he may have

165

been called in, should structural work be required or some planning issue need resolving.

I think these are the people I had discussed the Dalmannoch venture with, but of course word would have circulated round the brothers before Brother Richard's departure. It was not a secret."

The inspector thanked the prior for his openness and asked if he could meet with Brother Jacob, the only one, of those specifically mentioned by the prior, apart from the trustees, whom he had not previously met. This was granted and the two policemen were shown to the stores.

Brother Jacob was somewhat taken aback by the arrival of two Scottish policemen within his domain, but he was happy enough to reveal what he knew whether relevant or not to the investigation. He was, to be frank, a gossip.

The officers listened patiently to the ins and outs of his mother's illness and the fact that the prior had given him periodic leave of absence to visit her. Of more relevance to the case, Brother Jacob alluded to Brother's Richard's incident at Meadow View; he described the demands placed on him as store master to supply the tools and materials for the construction of the bell tower and the exacting stipulations of the architect Jamie Arbuckle, whom he seemed to resent.

Then there was the matter of obtaining a van. An uncle of Brother Jacob was a director of a car dealership called Abona Motors. Through this contact he had been able to purchase, for a good price, the Ford Transit van to be used by Brother Richard.

Inspector Morrison was beginning to tire of the rambling nature of Brother Jacob's account and interposed:

"Tell us about how you purchased the van."

"Well, you see," explained the monk, "my uncle put me on to one of the salesmen who was temporarily based at the Cheltenham branch of Abona Motors, a man called Gerald Flynn. I went over to the outlet in Cheltenham a couple of times to meet with him. He was very helpful and showed a lot of interest in the priory here and the work of the brothers. Of course I was able to tell him quite a lot and about the bell tower. We are very proud of the bell tower, you know. I have to say that Brother Richard did excellent work, although I was able to help and guide him quite a bit . . ."

The inspector interposed again:

"Did you mention Brother Richard's project at Dalmannoch to this Mr Flynn?

"Oh yes, I'm sure I did," confirmed Brother Jacob. "Oh yes. You see that was the reason we needed the van. In fact, now that I recall, he asked me where Dalmannoch was. Well I didn't know, but I found out and told him on my second visit to Cheltenham to pick up the van. It's funny Mr. Flynn had the appearance of a – how can I say – smooth operator, yet he had such interest in our work here. Shows you, doesn't it?"

The two policemen looked at each other, thinking the same thoughts. The inspector asked:

"Have you seen Gerald Flynn since then?"

"Oh, yes indeed," responded the monk, "he called here two or three times. He was interested to hear how Brother Richard was getting on. I told him that he phoned in every Sunday at lunch time after he had been to Mass at a place called St Aidan's."

The policemen looked at each other again.

"Could you give us your uncle's name please and his contact details?" was the next question by the inspector. After noting the answer, they thanked Brother Jacob for his time and departed from Whitleigh Priory.

The next call was the nearby Meadow View Home for the Elderly.

Sharon Wilkins, who had been given responsibility for managing the home, in Frances' absence, while anxious about Frances' welfare, was able to confirm how Brother Richard had rescued Frances from Gerry Flynn's assault, of Frances' subsequent flight, and of subsequent visits by Gerry.

"Right George," the inspector declared on leaving Meadow View, "Let's track down this Flynn character."

The two officers drove to the Bristol headquarters of Abona Motors where they met Bert Benson, a director of the firm and uncle of Brother Jacob, but an altogether harder nosed character.

"Gerry Flynn?" stated the director; "a good salesman, but unreliable, disappears without a 'by your leave' and then comes back with some cock-and-bull-story or another of an excuse, especially of late."

"We're keen to meet him," the inspector inquired, "Where can we find him?"

"God knows. Your guess is a good as mine," responded the hard bitten Bert, "He sold a nice black Mercedes C180 Kompressor a couple of days ago and took off on leave. He said he'd be back next week."

"Thank you for your help Mr Benson. Please let me know as soon as Mr Flynn returns. I believe he may have some valuable information for us."

On the drive back to Cirencester, the policemen reviewed the day's deliberations.

"George, I think we may hae found our man."

FRANCES' NIGHTMARE

THAT FLEETING MOMENT, when Frances recognised her husband at Garlieston pier, was the point at which she realised that Gerry had at last tracked her down. As she looked aghast, Gerry bolted before anyone had the presence of mind to stop him. The police car had meanwhile already begun to speed away from the pier with its unsavoury rucksack carrying passenger.

Catriona, however, took the initiative to phone the Galloway Divisional Command on her mobile to alert them as to the identity of Jamie Arbuckle's impersonator and the possibility that he might be Alexander Agnew's killer.

Once Brother Richard, Frances, Ruairidh and their legal friends disembarked from *Balmoral* they headed towards the village to retrieve their respective vehicles. It was about quarter to ten just as the sun was setting when Brother Richard and Frances reached Dalmannoch. They had scarcely time to put on the kettle when a police car drew up and two officers, a sergeant and a constable rang the door bell.

Brother Richard opened the door with a:

"Come in, we've just put on the kettle."

"That's all right Sir. We won't stop for long. Is Mrs. McGarrigle here?"

Frances appeared from the kitchen with a tray of tea cups, pot, milk, sugar and cake and invited the officers to take a seat in the common room. Notwithstanding their earlier protest, the officers accepted the beverages – and the cake.

"We just came to thank you, Mrs. McGarrigle, for alerting us to the suspected drug trafficker on the *Balmoral*. You'll understand I can't say too much at this stage but I can tell you that Ferdie's – em – the trafficker's rucksack was stuffed with high grade crack cocaine and he has been detained for questioning. We'd just like to take a statement from you as to how you jaloused[*] that the – em – suspect was in fact carrying drugs."

Frances outlined her husband's debt problems; how she had been running from him; how Inspector Morrison had agreed with the hypothesis that Gerry may have been drawn into the drug trade; how she had seen the unsavoury man arguing with her husband in Dublin, and how she had spotted the same man boarding the *Balmoral* at Douglas in the Isle of Man. Brother Richard then added that Betty McDowell had recognised Gerry at Garlieston pier as the man who had arranged to meet Alexander Agnew immediately prior to his death.

Such had been the speed of events that word of Gerry's association with Alexander Agnew had not by that stage reached the two officers. The sergeant scratched his head.

"Well, Imph'm, Aye. This is an important development right enough. Well need to report it to Divisional Command."

Frances informed the officers that this had been done less than an hour before by Catriona Macarthur and with that the policemen made their exit.

The next morning was Sunday and at around ten o' clock Gordon Douglas and Suzie Silver arrived.

---

[*] Jaloused: a Scots word meaning suspected or ascertained

"I hope you dinna mind," explained Gordon, more animated than usual, "but I've been warkin' oot a better heatin' system and I just want to check oot whaur I can mak some modifications tae the pipe-work. An' Suzie wants tae draa oot some decoration thochts she has."

The offer was readily agreed to. Gordon set about rummaging among the pipes in a kitchen press and Suzie sat with a sketch pad drafting out some interior design ideas. While this was going on, Brother Richard announced that he was off in the Renault on his now customary Sunday attendance at St Aidan's.

Not long after Richard's departure, Gordon declared that he too was going back with his van to his workshop in Newton Stewart to pick up some joints, valves and stop cocks.

For a short time the building was quiet until a silver BMW drew up. Frances opened the door. There stood a grim faced Gerry Flynn. He pushed his way into the hallway.

"Got you alone at last", he snarled, "You know why I'm here."

"I can guess", replied Frances, trying to hide her fear. "How did you know where I was?"

"I didn't until I saw you last night on the boat with that monk," retorted Gerry; "I put two and two together."

"If its money you're after," insisted Frances, "what I have is all tied up. I can't get ready access to it."

"Well it'll have to be untied. I'm still your husband. You can't hold out on me."

"Some husband; we're separated", snapped Frances. "I've told you I want nothing more to do with your violence; your gambling and spendthrift ways. I have a life to lead and you're not part of it."

Gerry was holding his temper, although clearly highly agitated. "The guys I owe are ruthless. If they can't get it from me, they'll sure as Hell get it from you."

"What have you done Gerry to get yourself, AND me, into this mess? I know all about Billy Wilson. He's got you involved in the drugs trade, hasn't he?" Frances couldn't hide her contempt for Gerry. "If so it's despicable – the misery it causes."

"I had no choice," Gerry whined and clenched his fists. "I would have been beaten to a pulp after they had taken everything I had off me if I hadn't agreed to handle his crack cocaine shipments from Ireland. The police and Customs are watching Holyhead and Fishguard like hawks. I've had to come up with new routes but that has misfired and got me in deeper debt. I'll be smashed to pieces and you will too unless you stump up. Billy's brother Jimmy is coming down from Glasgow right now. He's a thug. He's lost a packet on two runs recently and he's raging. I'm in the firing line and honey so are you."

Gerry had worked himself up into a frenzy and Frances backed away from him as he moved towards her. He grabbed her by the neck and pressed her against the panelled wall of the hallway.

"Now, I'm not messing about you bitch," he shouted; "you'll draw out eighty grand in cash and that will be that."

"Eighty thousand pounds," gasped Frances; "I can't lay my hands on that kind of money. Even if I could, today's Sunday. All the banks are shut."

Gerry punched her hard. Her mouth started to bleed.

"You will you bitch, you will – tomorrow – and you'll come with me now before your holy roller friend comes back. Oh yes I know he always goes to church at this time on Sundays. Oh yes, oh yes, I know a lot of things. I have my contacts at Whitleigh."

By this time Gerry was laughing maniacally and twisted Frances arm behind her back. "I'm not letting you out of my sight until I have the money. I'm taking you away until you can get your money paid out in cash. No matter how long it takes."

"Aahhh, your hurting me Gerry", Frances screamed.

"Not half as much as Jimmy Wilson will hurt you while he's waiting for payment", Gerry sneered.

"You're mad", screamed Frances struggling to try to free herself from Gerry's grip. "You murdered Alexander Agnew, didn't you? Right here at Dalmannoch."

Gerry stopped for a moment, surprised at this accusation. He protested:

"I didn't mean to kill him. I had to get Agnew to sell Dalmannoch to Teddy North. He's an associate of Jimmy Wilson. But he wouldn't co-operate – the stubborn fool – not even for ten thousand pounds. He said your damned holy roller monk, Brother Richard, was about to arrive. He'd only deal with him. I lost it and hit him with a stone. I didn't think . . . I didn't mean to hit him so hard. But, you know – ha ha – if I killed you – I'd inherit all your money, not just the measly eighty 'k' I need to pay off the Wilson Brothers."

Gerry seemed in a daze. Frances manage to struggle free and ran. Gerry lunged for her legs. She toppled and took a header for the common room door post. Bang ! – stars ! – blank . . .

173

SUZIE SILVER TAKES THE INITIATIVE

SUZIE SILVER was sitting at the kitchen table with her sketch pad, allowing her rich, extraordinary and magical imagination to conjure up dramatic but tasteful decorative schemes for the interior of a future Dalmannoch which, if fortune was kind, might become a centre for the Galloway Gaelic Group, the Wigtown Wicca Coven and perhaps other like minded and civilised people.

It was while she had started doodling out some very preliminary sketches that she heard voices in the hall – raised voices. She went to the door to investigate and heard Frances:

". . . drugs trade, hasn't he?" . . . If so it's despicable – the misery it causes."

And then a man's voice in a nasty tone:

"I had no choice," . . . "I would have been beaten to a pulp after they had taken everything I had off me if I hadn't agreed to handle his coke . . ."

Suzie was shocked. What was going on? Frances was obviously distressed and the man was clearly up to no good. She was about to go to Frances' aid, but stopped herself. Her sixth sense told her that this was really serious and more than she could cope with on her own. She pondered and then decided to slip away out of the back door to find reinforcements. She had the foresight to pick up the key for Brother Richard's Transit van from its hook as she departed.

As a dancer and naturally light of foot, she stepped round the side of the building and saw Gerry Flynn's silver BMW. Heart racing, she crept up to the car and looked in a window. The key was in the ignition.

Suzie gently opened the driver's door removed the key and pushed the door shut as quietly as she could.

She smiled a grim smile, that'll hold things up for a bit. As she prepared to head for the van she heard Frances scream:

"You're mad . . . You murdered Alexander Agnew, didn't you?"

This was really serious. There was neither landline telephone nor mobile phone reception at Dalmannoch, but she cursed the fact that she had left her own mobile behind on charge that morning. She ran as quietly as she could to Brother Richard's old Transit van, which was parked by the chapel facing down hill towards the drive. She climbed in, turned the ignition, but not as far as the self-start position, released the handbrake and the van started to roll silently down the drive, slowly at first then gathering speed until it was hidden from the house by the wood. At that point in the van's progress she started the engine and headed towards Wigtown.

She had driven Gordon's van a couple of times before but the Transit was bigger and seemed heavier to handle. Nevertheless she drove as fast as she could; lurching round bends as she tried to control the unfamiliar vehicle. In fifteen minutes she reached Elven Cottage, Thomas Nutter's house which was a couple of miles to the south of Wigtown. The van screeched to a halt, Suzie jumped out sprinted up Thomas' short front path, rang the bell and banged on the door.

"What's all the fuss and noise?" Thomas grumbled as he opened the door.

"Thomas," panted Suzie, "Frances is in trouble at Dalmannoch. The man who murdered Alexander Agnew is threatening her. We need to help."

"Slow down sister," Thomas gestured with his hands to calm Suzie, "Slow down. Elucidate – Frances? – Murder?"

Suzie summarised the situation at Dalmannoch, reminding Thomas as to who Frances was, and reminding him also of the, so far, unsolved murder of the lawyer, Alexander Agnew. Once he had a proper grasp of what was happening, Thomas paused for a few seconds then decided on a course of action.

"Right. Just as well it's a Sunday and Holly's here, to plan the Midsummer arrangements. We'll head for Dalmannoch in the Kombi. You phone the police from here and then phone Gordon. Once you have done that, both of you follow us. Pull the front door behind you when you leave. We'll try to hold this lunatic at bay until the police arrive."

With that Thomas and Holly puttered off in the extraordinary multi-coloured Volkswagen Kombi 'hippy van'.

Notwithstanding his somewhat comical name, Suzie had great respect for Thomas' capabilities. While he gave the impression of being a gentle, fair minded and somewhat mystical soul, he was in fact an ex marine and well able to handle himself and others in a crisis. Encouraged by this thought, Suzie took up the telephone receiver in the living room and dialled 999.

The experience was almost a repeat of Frances' of the previous evening:

"Hello . . . Yes. Police . . . Police? . . . This is very urgent. The man who murdered Alexander Agnew is at Dalmannoch and threatening our friend Frances McGarrigle . . . Yes I know because I heard him admitting the murder to Frances . . . Dalmannoch . . . It's in the Machars . . . The Machars – Galloway past

176

Wigtown and not as far as Whithorn . . . It's where Alexander Agnew was murdered. The police should know exactly where it is . . . My name? Susan Silver . . . Yes . . . I'm phoning from Elven Cottage near Wigtown . . . No. This is the home of Thomas Nutter . . . N U T T E R . yes . . . I was at Dalmannoch and overheard some of the conversation . . . No I'm not mistaken . . . No . . . Yes . . . I managed to slip away . . . Look this is very urgent . . . I'm fearful for Mrs McGarrigle's life . . . Please hurry . . . Yes this number . . . Thank you."

Suzie felt drained by the telephone conversation not least due to the feeling that the police telephonist seemed to doubt her report. She picked up the phone again and dialled the number for Gordon's workshop. The number rang out and the answering service kicked in. She left a message explaining the situation and the urgent need for Gordon to return to Dalmannoch.

She couldn't remember his mobile number so she phoned Douglas Gordon, who was fortunately at home.

"Duggie; have you got Gordon's mobile number? . . . Oh good . . . Thank you. We have a terrible crisis at Dalmannoch. The murderer of Alexander Agnew has turned up and he's threatening Frances . . . Yes he's there right now but I've removed his ignition key. Thomas; you know Thomas; Thomas Nutter and Holly Garden from the coven are heading over there right now. I'm to follow but I need to contact Gordon and get him to come too. Could you do that? . . Good. Then I'll go back to Dalmannoch right away . . . Yes I'll be careful. Don't worry."

Suzie replaced the receiver, pulled the front door behind her, climbed into the Transit, started it and headed back on the road to Dalmannoch. As she picked up speed she saw in her mirror a black car nosing out looking for an opportunity to pass. Then at a straight section of the road, a Mercedes Benz C180 Kompressor roared past. She continued in its wake until it was out of sight after a series of bends. She was finding the Transit heavy.

At last the Transit swung into the Dalmannoch entrance, up the drive through the wood and as the buildings came into view the silver BMW was still there; how could it be otherwise? Thomas' Kombi was parked by the chapel but parked between the two was the Black Mercedes.

SUZIE STOPPED THE TRANSIT beside the chapel and reversed it alongside the Kombi. There was nobody to be seen. She decided to slip round to the back of the building by passing round the side of the chapel. Crouching low she peered through the open kitchen window. She could hear voices from within. A rough Glasgow accent predominated.

"Flynn, ye're a f—in' eejit. First you bump off thon f—in' lawyer Agnew, and let doon Teddy North, now ye've f—in' killt yer wife before we got wur f—in' cash."

Then a different voice, English this time, "She's not dead, she's just stunned. It was an accident."

"Aye, accident," rejoined the Glasgow voice, "that's aw you're capable o' – f—in' accidents. Through your f—in' accidents aa've lost near enough a hunner f—in' grand. First Cairnryan and noo Garlies'. An accident ye've went an lost ye'r car key a suppose – ye f—in' eejit, so ye are. An noo an accident them f—in' weirdoes turnt up and nearly had you f—in' liftet. Just as well Billy and me came here when we did, so it is. Noo help me move the wumman intae the f—in' caur."

"I've hurt my hand", whined the English voice. "It got caught when she fell."

"Aw, ye f—in' pansy ye; use ye'r good haun. Come oan noo, Billy's got them weirdoes covered in the front room. He'll shoot if they make a move."

To Suzie, what the Glaswegian's vocabulary lacked in variety, it made up for in brute force. She was completely gob-smacked. It seemed as though Thomas and Holly were being held at gunpoint while the other

179

two men were intent on taking Frances into the car. Was she unconscious? How did that happen? Where exactly were Thomas and Holly? What was to be done to delay things until the police arrived?

There was no time to waste. A diversion. That was it. But how? What? Suzie slipped to the out buildings and rummaged for something to make a noise. Ah; a wash tub. That was a start – and then length of washing line; old fruit boxes and a scythe. She quietly set the tub filled with a metal watering can and other junk on two boxes just beside the row of out buildings. She then tied one end of the washing line through the slats of one of the boxes and payed it out to a vantage point by the corner of the back wing of the main Dalmannoch building. Then she quietly set up the scythe partially covered with strawberry netting on an orange box just by the back kitchen door such that the opening of the door would trigger its fall. Back and forward she scampered as quietly and as quickly as she could. It seemed like an age but the whole operation probably took less than five minutes.

Pausing a few seconds for breath, Suzie listened. There was an indistinct murmur of some discussion from one of the front rooms, and then:

"OK Flynn, we've wasted enough time, so we have. Let's get ye'r guid wumman movin'."

Suzie counted to five and threw a large stone through the kitchen window with a very satisfactory crashing of glass. She immediately withdrew to the corner of the back wing.

"What the f—in' Hell was that? Go an' have a look Flynn," came the Glasgow voice.

The said Flynn opened the back door, the scythe slewed downwards pulling the strawberry net with it and

180

tangling the individual up in such a way that the recently sharpened blade of the scythe cut his leg and the net caused him to trip and fall struggling forwards out of the kitchen and into the yard in a tangle crying out:

"Ow, aahh; oh I'm cut. oh Jesus – aahh !"

"What the f— noo !" the other shouted from inside the kitchen. And from her vantage point peeping round the corner of the back wing, Suzie saw an overweight man in a light grey shiny mohair suit, black shirt and silver tie stumble over the first man as he exited the kitchen door to further cries of:

"Ow, Jesus ! Oh, I'm bleeding !"

"Aw shut ye'r face ye f—in' nyaff. Look at my guid troosers, they've went an' got tore."

As the hullabaloo died down and the two men started to pick themselves up Suzie pulled the washing line with the result that a crash and assorted jangles were heard from the direction of the out buildings.

"For f—s sake there's somebody up there in thon sheds. C'mon"

At this Suzie ran round to the front of the building, another stone in hand. She quickly looked in the windows of the dining room and reception but there was no one there. She approached the front door very cautiously. It was open. She peeped round the edge of the door and saw Frances lying on the hall floor, lifeless. Then she spotted the gunman, Billy they had called him, standing by the common room door, looking uneasily and alternately into the room and towards the kitchen.

Then he spotted Suzie. She bolted and ran towards the cars. He rushed to the front door took his automatic in both hands, aimed and fired but missed as Suzie made cover behind the BMW. As Billy moved towards the car, gun in hand, Thomas surged from the common room and with a running Rugby tackle grounded him. The two men struggled for possession of the gun.

Billy was the stronger of the two and after the initial shock of the fall had managed to get on top of Thomas but couldn't quite bring the automatic to bear. Thomas, although long out of military service was the abler fighter and kneed Billy in the groin so getting the upper hand. He had just managed to wrest the gun from Billy when a voice rasped:

"Don't move a muscle or I'll blow ye'r f—in' brains oot." It was the Jimmy now holding a gun to Thomas' head.

Thomas let go of his quarry and his automatic and was kicked aside by Billy's rescuer.

"Thank f— for that Jimmy. I thought I was done for." Gasped Billy.

"Ye should be more careful. Ye've been too long away from Gleska[*]. Noo let's get this creep back inside. Tie him up this time and gie him a good kickin'."

As the two hoods started to bundle Thomas back to the common room, they realised that during the skirmish, Holly, now together with Suzie, had escaped from Billy's supervision.

On realising this, Jimmy recognised that things were getting out of hand.

"We'd better get tae f— out of here.

They had left it too late. Two police cars sirens blaring stormed up the drive towards the house.

Billy and Jimmy followed by a limping Gerry Flynn pushed Thomas at gunpoint towards the Mercedes.

---

[*] Glasgow

The police cars screeched to a halt. Out of the leading car emerged Inspector Morrison and Sergeant Watt. Two other officers alighted from the second car. The officers were unarmed. They had not expected such violent members of the Glasgow criminal fraternity to be present in this quiet part of Galloway.

Inspector Morrison approached the gang.

"All right; that's enough. Drop your weapons. You don't want to add murder to your charges.

"No f—in' way," replied Jimmy defiantly, sneering at the gathering audience, "I'll shoot this f—er unless you let us drive off."

"Now don't be a fool," the inspector cajoled, "You'll not get away with this. Give yourselves up."

As Inspector Morrison talked, Sergeant George Watt had worked his way round the back of the Mercedes, judged his moment and ran at Jimmy, knocking him to the ground. His gun sent flying. Billy, however, spun around and fired at the sergeant. The bullet penetrated the policeman's shoulder. The sergeant fell but in that moment Inspector Morrison managed to overpower Billy with a punch in the stomach.

In the meleé Jimmy's automatic had landed at Gerry's feet. He stared at it – hesitated – bent down and picked it up. He took the pistol in both hands and took aim at the inspector.

A distant shot rang out. Gerry grimaced, slumped and fell to the ground. Blood oozed from his chest. He was dead.

FOR A FEW SECONDS there was a stunned silence. Then the police rushed in. Jimmy and Billy Wilson were cuffed and, once a police van had arrived after a radio message had requested this facility, they were taken away to face the full rigour of Scots law.

The source of the shot that had killed Gerry soon became manifest. The driver of a grey mud splattered Land Rover Discovery, which had come though the Dalmannoch Wood, had stopped on seeing an array of police and other vehicles. He had detected an imminent tragedy. That man was Hector Woodrow-Douglas, who had returned from an early morning's stalking of roe deer on a cousin's land. With him were Professor Ruairidh Alasdair Macdonald and Douglas Gordon.

The Chief of the Green Douglasses, had retrieved his faithful Remington 700 rifle from its case in the back of his cousin's vehicle and rested his elbow on the bonnet. He took careful aim through the telescopic sight at the man who had picked up a hand gun and pointed it at a policeman, squeezed the trigger and found his mark.

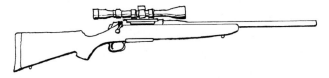

Hector Woodrow-Douglas' Remington 700

He waited there briefly, in case there was any further need for his services. But once the police had got things under control, he replaced the rifle in its case, resumed the driving seat and proceeded onward such that the vehicle's occupants were able join the assembled company.

Inspector Morrison's first action was to go to the aid of his doughty injured sergeant who was holding his blood stained left shoulder.

"How is it George?"

"Aw no too bad. It's gey sair – but – ah can move ma airm."

Relieved that the wound was not more serious, another officer took charge of the sergeant's welfare.

Inspector Morrison then went over to meet the new arrivals.

"Ah. Professor Macdonald, to whom do I give thanks for saving my life?"

"Not me, I'm afraid," the professor advised; "It was Mr Woodrow-Douglas here."

"Well," said the inspector, with much admiration for the new arrival; "All I can say is: 'good shot' and thank you."

"Don't mention it," retorted Hector, "I had better luck just now, than I did earlier this morning. We never got a single buck."

"By the way," asked the inspector, reverting to official mode; "You do have a license for that rifle?"

"Since I was knee high to a grasshopper," was the clan chief's cheery answer.

Attention now turned to Frances. Holly, who was a nurse by training, was already kneeling over the unconscious woman testing her pulse and mopping her brow.

"She's coming round. Bring a glass of water and get a pillow."

Suzie hurried to the kitchen and brought back the requested drink and then rushed upstairs to come back with two pillows. Everyone gathered round concerned about the innocent victim of the morning's confrontations.

A little moan emitted from Frances' lips; she moved her head a little, moaned again and opened her eyes.

"What happened? – where? – Gerry? – oo my head?

"It's all right. Don't worry. Gerry's not here. You're safe, sip this." Holly soothed the concussed sister – a fellow colleague in need.

"Where's Richard?" was Frances' next question.

"He'll soon be here my lass." And as Holly spoke the Renault drew up to join the growing number of vehicles. Brother Richard stepped out looking puzzled at the assembled crowd.

"Hello what's going on?"

Then he saw Gerry's body still lying near the front door at the spot he had seen the body of Alexander Agnew exactly a month before,.

"What's happened?"

He looked from one to the other, bewildered, and his eyes fell on Frances lying propped up in the hallway. He knelt by her side, held her hand, tears falling from his eyes. He whispered:

"Oh my God, my love, my beautiful Frances; what has happened to you?"

She smiled:

"I'm not quite sure." She was still in a dreamy daze. "Gerry was here, but he's gone. And now you're here. Everything'll be alright."

And so it was.

An ambulance was summoned on the inspector's car radio.

While they awaited its arrival, Gordon's van turned up and Suzie ran over to meet her overdue boy friend.

"What kept you? You've missed all the action."

He had decided to pre-assemble some pipe work and Newton Stewart was a fair drive away and he hadn't been away much more than an hour, but then looking around, he asked in his lugubrious way:

"What action?"

There ensued a babble of explanations. No single person knew the full story but bit by bit, the saga was untangled. They heard how Gerry had arrived and pressed Frances for money; how Suzie had overheard enough to realise that Frances was in danger and had gone for help; how Thomas and Holly had arrived and found Frances unconscious and had been on the point of apprehending Gerry when the Wilson brothers had arrived and had turned the tables on them. It was Suzie's arrival and her diversionary tactics and Thomas' assailing of Billy that had allowed the others to escape pending the arrival of the police. Finally everyone was reminded that, had it not been for the marksmanship of Hector Woodrow Douglas, the whole affair might have ended very differently.

Frances had been trying to take all this in but was confused.

"What did Hector do?"

Holly held Frances' hand and mopped her brow and, as comfortingly as she could, she said.

"He shot Gerry. Gerry's dead."

Frances took in this news and frowned a little. She sighed.

"I'm glad. God forgive me."

Brother Richard took her hand.

"Your troubles are all over now my love. I'll look after you and cherish you and keep you from hurt. You see if I don't. And, you know, you have an awful lot of good friends here. See how they have protected you from terrible evil. I'm so grateful to them all."

Frances looked at him, gave a weak but heartfelt smile and she squeezed her beloved monk's hand.

He turned to Suzie, Thomas and Holly.

"What can I say to thank you all."

Thomas then turned to Suzie and declared:

"Suzie Silver was the heroine of the moment. Without her initiative, bravery and ingenuity; evil would have had its way."

Suzie blushed and for the first time that day wasn't quite sure what to do. Then she pondered and, after a bit, she smiled and announced:

"Brother Richard, I'm honoured that we Pagans were able to come to Frances' rescue. We like her very much and, as Holly explained to you when we first visited you, we believe in the complementarity of the benevolent and the malignant and in the Law of the Threefold Return. Evil was done to Frances by one individual and three evil doers have suffered as a consequence. On behalf of the coven, I would ask one thing of you. It is this. May we hold out midsummer sabbat here at Dalmannoch.

Brother Richard looked at each of them and at Hector, Ruairidh, Douglas, Gordon, Inspector Morrison at Sergeant Watt supported by two other officers, and at Frances. He raised one eyebrow and smiled.

"I could hardly refuse, could I ?"

POSTSCRIPT

IT MAY BE ENQUIRED what became of Frances, Brother Richard, their new found friends and of Dalmannoch after that fateful Sunday morning.

Once the ambulance arrived, Frances and Sergeant Watt were taken to hospital. Both were kept in overnight but allowed out the following day. Frances suffered intermittent headaches for a couple of weeks but recovered from her ordeal rapidly thereafter. She tendered her resignation to the Meadow View Home for the Elderly but went back there for a month to arrange for hand over to a new manager-in-chief. Fortuitously the new incumbent was none other than Sharon Wilkins, the senior care assistant, who had ably held the fort in Frances' absence. During that short spell at Meadow View, Frances met Darren Williams, whilst on a visit to his grandfather, Tom Bayliss. It seemed that Darren was a changed young man; training hard having been selected to play in the district league. By the beginning of August, Frances was back at Dalmannoch.

For the two weeks after the death of Gerry Flynn, Brother Richard had looked after Frances, although it has been argued that it was she who looked after him. He had decided that he would not pursue his life as a monk at Whitleigh Priory but he returned to the Cotswolds with Frances for a few days to meet with Prior John, collect his few worldly possessions and bid a very fond farewell to his brothers. On leaving the priory, Richard paid a visit to his aunt and uncle in Brixham and some other relations in Cornwall. He then returned to Dalmannoch which had been left meantime under the temporary care of Suzie and Gordon.

Suzie briefly became something of a local celebrity, featuring in a relatively accurate article in the *Galloway Gleaner* penned by Jock the Shock. She commenced on an imaginative decorative scheme for the interior of the main Dalmannoch building that later received favourable comment in one of the quality interior design magazines.

The legalities of transferring the Dalmannoch buildings and land from the old Dalmannoch Trust to a new Dalmannoch not-for-profit Company commenced almost immediately and the conveyance was completed shortly after Richard's return north. Hector Woodrow Douglas put up the bulk of the capital in return for which he was allocated, for his exclusive use, a comfortable upstairs suite in the main building. There were also contributions from other bodies and a long term loan of £100,000 from Frances.

It may, or may not, come as a surprise that Catriona Macarthur and Robert Heron became close friends and, although there is a considerable age difference between them, there is speculation that an engagement may be expected. The memory of their late friend and colleague Alexander Agnew was marked on a plaque by an oak tree sapling planted in the Dalmannoch grounds shortly after change of ownership.

All in all, after the deal was concluded, Whitleigh Priory was the recipient of £612,000. In gratitude Prior John Ainslie wrote the following letter to Richard.

Dear Richard,

I am writing to you to express my heartfelt thanks for your very considerable enterprise and fortitude in achieving the transfer of the financial assets of the Dalmannoch Trust to Whitleigh Priory. I am well aware of the daunting challenges both physical and spiritual that you faced in achieving this end and respect you all the more for that.

I understand, albeit with regret, that you have decided that the calling of a monk is not for you and that you will be striking out on a new and I am sure fulfilling path in a worldlier sphere. Your contribution towards the development of Whitleigh Priory has been immense, bearing in mind the short time you have been with us, and you will be sorely missed.

I know the brothers will all wish you God's blessing for your future, as do I, and remember, you will always remain our brother and will find a welcome here.

God be with you.

John

Richard was heartened and relieved to read this letter. He maintained a strong affection for Whitleigh Priory and was glad that his departure and his commitment to Frances had left no bad taste.

Billy and Jimmy Wilson were a different matter. They were convicted on multiple charges of which extortion and attempted abduction were but a part. They were incarcerated at Her Majesty's pleasure for eight and ten years respectively. The man with the rucksack, Ferdie Muldoon was small fry by comparison and he got three years. Teddy North was charged with corruption and got off with a deferred sentence. His business empire collapsed and he faded from view.

Sergeant George Watt's nasty flesh wound healed quickly and some time later he was awarded the Queen's Gallantry Medal for his valour in preventing the escape of the Wilson Brothers. He wears the blue, silver and red ribbon with the same pride with which he speaks his Scots tongue.

It may finally be wondered if Brother Richard, Frances, the Galloway Gaelic Group, the Pagans, Professor Macdonald and others found a future at Dalmannoch. Well of course they did, but that is another story.

THE END ?

GLOSSARY OF SCOTS AND GAELIC WORDS AND EXPRESSIONS

The Scots language, or Broad Scots, is characterised by a variety of regional dialects. The somewhat different usages of Galloway and Glasgow feature in the affair of Brother Richard. The Gaelic languages of Ireland, Scotland and the Isle of Man are distinct languages. They are, however, sufficiently closely related that, with a little of effort, a degree of mutual comprehension is possible. The glossary below lists the Gaelic and Scots words and phrases that appear in this book with linguistic differentiation indicated as follows:
IG = Irish Gaelic; MG = Manx Gaelic; S = Scots; SG = Scottish Gaelic

Aa (S) I, all
Aboot (S) about
A ghràidh (SG) love
Agus (IG & SG) and
Ain (S) own
Ar ais go (IG) back to
An (S) and
Anseo (IG) here
Aw (S) all
Awa (S) away
Aye (S) yes, always
Bail ó Dhia ort (IG) a term of affection and welcome, *lit.* Condition from God on you
Bairn (S) child
Baith (S) both
Ben (S) through, inside the house
Bit (S) but

Bittie (S) smallish part (OF)
Brither (S) Brother
Boondary (S) boundary
Buail isteach (IG) pop in(side)
Caad (S) called**Canna** (S) can't
Caur (S) car
Cèilidh (SG) visit, musical event
Chan eil dona (SG) not bad
Ciamar a tha thu? (SG) How are you?
C'mon (S) come on
Cooncil (S) council
Coorse (S) course
Crack (S) amiable conversation
Dae (S) do
Dinna (S) don't
Doon (S) down
Doot (S) doubt
Draa (S) draw, sketch
Dys (MG) to
Eejit (S) idiot, fool
Een (S) eyes
(h)Éirin (IG) Ireland
Fae (S) from
Fear and taighe (SG) master of ceremonies
Failt ort (MG) Welcome (on you)
Fáilte romhat (IG) Welcome to you
Fairm (S) farm
Fastyr mie (MG) good afternoon
Faur (S) far
G(h)allghaidhealaibh (SG) Galloway
Gàidhlig (SG) Gaelic language
Gey (S) very
Gie (S) give
Gin (S) if

195

Gleska (S) Glasgow
Grunnan (SG) group, cluster
Guid (S) good
Guid-wife (S) wife
Hae, hid (S) have, had
Haun (S) hand
Havna (S) have not
Haiverin' (S) speaking nonsense
His tae (S) has to
Hoo (S) how
Hoolie (S) rumpus, party
Ho ro gheallaidh (SG) party, soiree
Hotchin (S) abounding in
Intae (S) into
Jaloused (S) suspected, ascertained
Jist (S) just
Ken (S) know
Killt (S) killed
Laddie (S) boy (affectionate)
Lang (S) long
Ledy-frien (S) lady-friend
Liftet (S) arrested
Mannin (MG) the Isle of Man
Math d'fhaicinn (SG) good to see you
Mo croí (IG) (of) my heart
Muckle (S) much
Nae (S) no, not
No (S) not
Noo (S) now
Nyaff (S) a conceited but insignificant person
O' (S) of
Oan (S) on
Och (S) *interj* expressing regret
Onie (S) any

Oor (S) our
Oot (S) out
Ower (S) over, regarding
Pey (S) pay
Press (S) cupboard
Pun (S) pound(s)
Richt (S) right, proper, correct
Roon (S) around
Sláinte (IG) health
Slán (IG) Cheerio, goodby
Siller (S) silver, money
Tae (S) to
T(h)aisce (IG) treasure, darling
Tak (S) take
Tha thu fhein gu math (SG) you're well yourself
The day (S) today
Thochts (S) thoughts
Thon (S) those, yonder
Troosers (S) trousers
Turnt (S) turned
Twa (S) two
Verra (S) very
Warkin (S) working
Weel (S) well
Went (S) gone
Whit (S) what
Wi (S) with
Wid (S) would
Wiz (S) was
Wumman (S) woman
Wur (S) our
Ye (S) you
Yer (S) your

WHAT NEXT ?

If you enjoyed *Dalmannoch – The Affair of Brother Richard*, don't keep it a secret. Tell your friends.

If you would like to know what happens next in the affairs of Brother Richard, Frances McGarrigle, the professor, the Pagans, the Galloway Gaelic Group, and of new colourful characters, a second Dalmannoch story is in preparation. It's called *The Elven Knights Mystery*. Here is the first chapter:

THE DEAD RESEARCHER

NORMALLY, end of term was a time for rejoicing at the MacPhedran Institute of Celtic Studies. This year too, rejoicing would have been in order, had things been normal. In the course of his able leadership, Professor Ruairidh Alasdair Macdonald had seen a steady rise in student numbers and exam results were on the right side of the trend. But this year was not normal. Money was tight. He was in the financial firing line.

"Let there be no mistake; its make or break. Either income from research, or conferences, or other sources will have to rise, or savings will have to be made". Such was the ultimatum of Howard Winkley; the university's bursar. He added: "I have just returned from a seminar on university finance in Glasgow and let me say; if the institute doesn't improve its performance, drastic measures will follow."

Located in a converted rambling terraced house in one of the older parts of the Highland capital of Inverness, the formerly independent and struggling institute was established in 1928 by the late Aeneas MacPhedran, the celebrated Celtic scholar. The establishment was now a partner in a confederation of colleges and research institutions scattered throughout the vast Highlands and Islands of Scotland. If the MacPhedran Institute survived, it was to be re-located on a spanking new campus on the edge the pleasant, prosperous and burgeoning city. If not . . .

It was half past three as he saw the bursar out. The dismal Howard was always inclined to lay it on a bit thick. For sure the financial situation was worrying. To be more positive, however, the professor's research work in Galloway, in the far south west of Scotland, looked as though it might be close to bearing fruit with the potential for a series of prestigious and profitable international conferences in the offing.

The professor comforted himself further in that at least it was Friday and for once he had no evening or week-end work commitments. A few routine matters to attend to and he could be off home to his wife and family.

He leaned back in his swivel chair, gazed upwards at the cracked ceiling plaster and grimaced. He lowered his eyes again, sighed deeply to relieve the irritation he always felt after a meeting with 'that obnoxious wee man' who seemed to delight in bearing bad news.

His hand stretched out to pick up a silver framed photograph on his desk. He inspected it fondly. It was of a smiling group, featuring himself and others standing outside of what looked like a Victorian shooting lodge – Dalmannoch – which had become the hub of his southern endeavour. As the tension ebbed away, he, recalled with pleasant amazement how this project had emerged following a chance encounter, a year before, with a young monk called Brother Richard Wells and of the bizarre chain of events that had brought about a network of productive contacts and the creation of this outpost for the institute in that remote and unlikely rural area.

Since then, the Dalmannoch building was increasingly used by local groups and individuals. More importantly, from his professor's perspective; things were now starting to come together on the academic front. Good links were developing with universities, institutions and groups within and outside Scotland.

One of the first practical initiatives to emerge out of the evolving academic effort at Dalmannoch was a post-graduate research proposal by one Colin McCulloch. Admittedly Colin was an odd-ball – a loner, not easy to relate to, but unquestionably very bright intellectually. It was not that his unkempt appearance was a matter for comment; there were many, even within the staff of the college network, whose standard of dress was, to put it mildly, casual. It was an attitude thing. Aloof, sneering, sarcastic, judgemental and yet at times engaging, quick witted, amusing; the problem most people had in dealing with him was his unpredictability – not knowing how next the wind was going to blow.

The important thing about Colin, however, so far as Professor MacDonald was concerned, was an understanding of Galloway's early medieval history and archaeology, equal in depth to many acclaimed scholars twice his age. In particular it was Colin's ground-breaking insights into the relationship between Paganism and Christianity during that distant and ill-recorded Dark Age period which especially excited the professor. This was an area of research that he himself had been pursuing and in which he perceived an increasing international curiosity. And it was out of this international curiosity that Professor MacDonald saw future income generation and the financial saviour of the institute.

Thus, out of a strong mutual professional interest, and almost blind to their differences, an effective and even intense working relationship had been forged between the genial, cultivated professor and the disagreeable, anti-social researcher.

And now Colin was on the verge of something big; something to do with a mysterious group he had called the 'Elven Knights'. All was to be revealed in a pre-arranged phone call at four o' clock.

The phone rang. The professor picked up the receiver.

"Yes Jean ? . . The police ? . . Yes, of course, send them up to my room".

Half a minute later a police sergeant and a constable presented themselves.

"Good afternoon sir. You are Professor Ruairidh MacDonald ?"

"Yes, I am"

The sergeant held up a sheet of paper with a scanned copy of a business card that the professor recognised as his own.

"And is this your card ?"

"Well yes, it certainly looks like mine."

"Do you know, or know of, a Colin McCulloch ?"

"Yes I do, he's a research fellow with this institute. In fact I'm expecting a phone call from him any minute. Why do you ask ? Is there a problem ?

"I'm afraid there is Professor Macdonald. The Dumfries and Galloway police have just informed us that the body of Colin McCulloch has been found in a place near Dumfries called Sweetheart Abbey. He was stabbed to death."

To find out more reserve your copy from:

Pedersen
Lochlann
8 Drummond Road
Inverness
IV2 4NA

Email: roy@pedersen.org.uk

FOR THE RIGHT REASONS

This book is printed and bound by 'For the Right Reasons'; a volunteer run charity located in the Merkinch area of Inverness. It works to help people who want to conquer their life-wrecking drug or alcohol dependency. The project gives unconditional, un-judgemental support and friendship from the time a personal commitment is made to get clean, to the point of employment and re-integration with society.

Inverness is a prosperous and thriving city; yet within its bounds, Merkinch is one of the most deprived in Scotland. With a population of around 4,000, around 300 people are dependent on alcohol and about 150 dependent on opiates. Of these a growing number are teenagers. The social cost of these addictions is enormous.

As part of its rehabilitation programme, 'For the Right Reasons' operates three social enterprises in printing, publishing and recycling. The earnings from these, together with grants and donations enable the project to carry out its programme.

If you would like to fight for freedom from opiates by making a donation, go to:

www.fortherightreasons.org.uk
email: info@fortherightreasons.org.uk
For the Right Reasons
Printer & Publisher
60 Grant street
Inverness
IV3 8BN